Death by the Arno

Justin Ellis

Copyright © 2016 Justin Ellis

All rights reserved. No part of this publication may be copied, reproduced, stored in a retrieval system or transmitted in any form or by any means without the prior written permission of the author. Nor may it be circulated in any form, under any binding or cover, other than that in which it is published, without the prior written permission of the author.

ISBN: 1530866367
ISBN-13: 978-1530866366
BISAC: Fiction / Historical / General

DRAMATIS PERSONAE

Donato – a young artist from Lucca
Lodovico Corsini – a successful Florentine businessman
Giovanni Anziani – a minor artist
Grazia – Anziani's wife
Marco and Silvio – young brothers, petty criminals
The Prior – the Prior of San Miniato al Monte church
Piero Soderini – the *Gonfaloniere*, governor of Florence
Messer Pitti – a wealthy Florentine
Niccolò Machiavelli – a politician
Captain Scalieri – captain of the guard at the Palazzo della Signoria
Tedesco – a guard at the Palazzo della Signoria
Captain Giannini – captain of the City police
Federico Benvenuti – a businessman from northern Italy
Chiara – Benvenuti's daughter
Leonardo Vinci – artist, inventor, engineer
Michelangelo Buonarroti – artist
Gianluca Galeazzo – a merchant from Milan

Readers will notice that many aspects of life in Florence five hundred years ago are reflected in life today. Any similarity, however, between characters in this book and any modern person is entirely coincidental. Almost all of the historical events and characters in this book, apart from the main story-line, are accurately portrayed.

CHAPTER 1

Domes and spires stood on a bank of mist, unconnected with the earth beneath. This was how the City of Florence first greeted Donato's eyes when he rounded a bend in the track above the River Arno. He must have been walking for a couple of hours since sunrise. The vapour that had crawled up from the river on the typically chill March morning was starting to burn off but it was still thick enough to obscure the City at ground level.

Donato crouched down and picked up a handful of dirt. It hardly seemed possible that these stones and dust could become the giant structures he now saw ahead of him. Rich families had built some impressive towers in Lucca, from where he had left his own family home two days previously, but nothing to compare with these.

He was jolted back to reality by the sound of horses thundering along the track behind him. Donato turned around to see four mercenary soldiers charging towards him. He leapt backwards off the track to avoid being trampled, landing in a shallow ditch, up to his ankles in cold muddy water.

The soldiers sped past him in a cacophony of hooves and swords rattling in their scabbards. They looked ravaged by battle, but it was impossible to tell who they had been fighting for or against, as a thick layer of filth covered any colours they may have been wearing.

The riders disappeared in a cloud of dust, apparently ignorant of Donato's presence. He cursed them under his breath, climbed out of the ditch and took off his mud-caked shoes. He did not want to enter Florence looking like one of the many wandering mad-men that he had encountered on his way. For one thing, in a city with such a cultured reputation as Florence's he feared he might be locked up for being in such a state.

Donato looked towards the City once more. Although he had never been this far east before, he knew what some of the buildings were from drawings he had studied in Lucca's civic library. The great dome, with its fresh terra-cotta tiles glowing bright orange in the sunlight above the mist, must be the crowning glory of the Basilica di Santa Maria del Fiore, Florence's cathedral, which had been completed by one of Donato's heroes, Filippo Brunelleschi, seventy years ago.

Donato remembered reading how the cathedral had been open to the elements for a hundred years before that while the great artists, architects and engineers of the age tried to work out how to put an unsupported dome on top of such a wide circle without it falling in on itself. Brunelleschi had come up with his solution after studying the dome of the Pantheon built by the Ancient Romans in their capital. How strange, thought Donato, that Italy was only just catching up with where it had been more than a thousand years ago.

Next to the dome was Giotto's green, white and pink bell-tower. Not far to the right of that was a more spindly and severe stone tower which Donato guessed must be the top of the Palazzo della Signoria, the palace that housed the City's government. His mind's eye rushed forward to explore the cobbled alleyways that must lie behind the mist, dark from the shadows of the mighty buildings that loomed over them.

He decided to cross the lush meadow that sloped down the hill, covered in spring flowers, to reach the river whose course he had been following since the previous afternoon. Donato stripped off and waded in to wash the grime of the journey away down the river, in the direction he had just come from. The water was breathtakingly cold, having come down from the Apennine mountains where the winter snows were melting away, but Donato enjoyed its refreshing bite.

He gave his shoes a good wash, then laid them on a rock in the hope that they might dry a little in the watery sunshine. By the time Donato climbed out, the last fingers of mist had released their grip on the land and were retreating back into the river. He laid down on the grassy bank and let the victorious sun bring some warmth back to his naked body.

Once dry, Donato put his clothes back on and ate the last of the bread that he carried in his bag. He would need to find work quickly when he got into the City, to earn some money to pay for food and somewhere to stay.

His father had told him many times how their family had once been rich, but they had been reduced to poverty by the wars and plagues that had afflicted the land for the last two hundred years. Donato counted himself as one of the lucky ones – unusually, none of his family had died from those causes during his life-time. The government of Lucca had, however, appropriated half of their agricultural holdings, and a large portion of the little money that they made from the sale of their remaining crops disappeared in taxes to fund the city's ever-growing defences against its marauding neighbours.

Donato now heard bells striking from the towers he had been admiring before, calling the faithful to church for morning mass. By now the sun had climbed higher into the sky and was hot on his face. He got up, put on his still damp shoes, and walked along the riverbank until he reached the enormous wall, which gave the City an air of total impregnability.

Donato felt like turning back – how would he even survive in a place that was so clearly reluctant to welcome outsiders, let alone make a success of himself? But he persuaded himself that if he went into the City now, at least most people would be at church so he should be able to find himself a good vantage point from which to observe before they poured back out on to the streets. If he could just watch the locals for a while, he might feel more comfortable about being in their midst.

So he approached the gate nearest to the river, passing the stinking carcass of an over-worked donkey being picked apart by hungry crows. The rotten stench rising from the animal's body, combined with Donato's apprehension, almost made him retch. When he reached the gate, three guards stood in his way. One of them asked him "Where are you going?" in a tone that told Donato that his answer wasn't going to matter much

Donato declared with as much enthusiasm as he could muster "I am an artist, and I have come to work in the City." He could hear the nervous tremor in his voice, and knew that the guards would object. Florence had been the artistic centre of Europe for the past century, although the last ten years of upheaval had not done its reputation any good. The guards were used to artists coming to the City looking for employment. Most of them failed and ended up working as labourers in the textile or building trades.

"Too many of your lot here already" the guard said. "There aren't enough palaces left for you to decorate, they've all been done already. This is 1504, not 1404." The guards cast a smirk at each other. "What else can you do?"

"I've worked on building sites too," said Donato.

"Don't make me laugh. You're as thin as a grass-snake, you've never laid a brick in your life. How old are you?"

"Nineteen, and I have studied both painting and architecture for the past five years."

"Well we've got enough builders as well. Do you have letters of recommendation?" The City was expanding rapidly, and had become a dangerous place. Its guards had been ordered not to let strangers into the City unless sure that they were of sound character.

Donato fumbled in his bag, then mumbled that he must have lost his letters on the way. "You've come to

Florence to cash in on our success, but there isn't space for any more like you. Go back to wherever it is you came from," the guard sneered dismissively.

Donato tried pleading, but soon realised they were not going to let him in, whatever he said. He was disconsolate, never having even considered that a City this big would not allow people in freely, especially if they had a skill to share. But he wasn't ready to give up - he knew it was the right place for him, that it was his destiny to be there, no matter how forbidding it seemed. His ancestors had been Florentine, before they moved to Lucca as part of the army that occupied the small city-state in the *trecento*, the 1300s. He would have to bide his time, and sneak into the City somehow without the guards seeing him.

He walked along the outside of the wall, dwarfed by the imposing sheet of solid stone towering above him. There was a regular flow of traffic through the Porta al Prato, one of the main gates in the wall. Perhaps he could hide in one of the carts on its way into the City, laden with farm produce. But he saw that the guards were checking all carts before allowing entry, and realised it would not be that easy.

Once again, his hope started to waiver. Had he made a mistake coming here? Ok, so these were difficult times, but the security was surprisingly tight. Donato decided to wait until the cover of night. In the meantime, he would do his observing from the outside. He withdrew to sit between a couple of large rocks that lay about a hundred paces from the gate and gave him a little protection from the chilly afternoon breeze.

Carts went into the City piled high with winter

vegetables and early spring flowers, and hay stored from the previous year's harvest. Those leaving the City were either bare, returning to the farms that they had come from, or loaded up with the output of the City's craftsmen and women. Surly mercenaries came and went, looking busy but only occasionally having anything to show for their efforts, such as prisoners captured and accused of being spies for the Medici or some other faction.

Ordinary towns-people seemed to be able to leave and enter the City without having to go through the interrogation that Donato had been put to, and he guessed that the residents must all be known by face at least to the guards on their local gates. This only added to his sense of Florence being a closed community that he was going to find it hard to break into, both physically and socially.

As evening came, traffic into the City reduced. The produce crossing the gates in both directions virtually ceased, as cart-owners feared attack by bandits on the roads outside the City after nightfall. Once total darkness had enveloped the countryside outside the gates, Donato could see the light flickering above the wall from torches flaming in the City, and he could hear laughter and music rising from the houses of those fortunate enough to own property there. One day, I will be one of them, Donato told himself more out of hope than conviction.

Since few people tried to get into or out of the City after sunset, the number of guards reduced – most of them retreated to the warmth and wine of the guard-houses built into the City wall next to each gate. Thanks to the strength of its defences, it would take a whole army to attack the City, so when there was no military activity reported in the vicinity, the night-guard only had to operate a skeleton staff. Occasionally a group of brigands might try to break into the City, but the guard-houses could be quickly mobilised to cut them down.

* * * * *

Donato had been sitting still for a good while since darkness had fallen. The temperature had dropped considerably, and Donato was becoming desperate for shelter against the cold air of the dead of night. On his way from Lucca, he'd managed to find deserted animal sheds to rest in overnight and avoid the early morning frost, but the land around the City walls had been largely cleared of construction so that invaders could be spotted before they got near.

A cart, pulled by two oxen and laden with hay, lumbered along the road towards the gate. He did not want to risk hiding in the hay, because he had seen guards sinking their swords into similar cargoes to check for hidden passengers. If they killed someone, the guards did not care. If they caught an illicit intruder alive, they often killed him anyway, assuming him to be a spy. Without any real idea of what he might do next, he silently crept up behind the cart.

The gate had torches hung from the walls, which shed enough light for Donato to see the solitary guard stepping forward to the left of the oxen to speak to the driver of the cart, without being seen himself. The guard stopped the cart, and nattered to its driver for what seemed like eternity. Donato crouched on the opposite side. With the gate still shut, Donato could do nothing but wait and hope that an opportunity to slip through would come. Eventually the guard started to walk around the cart to check all was in order. Donato slid round the back of the cart to the other side then realised he had nowhere to go – if he carried on to the front, the driver would spot him and alert the soldier.

The oxen were restless, and their hooves digging at the dusty road made enough noise to allow Donato to crawl under the cart without being heard, just as the guard came round the back corner. The guard jumped up on to the cart and checked the load with deep thrusts of his sword. Finding nothing untoward, he got back down and completed the circuit, then banged loudly on the wooden gate with the butt of his sword for his colleague inside to open up before shouting to the driver to proceed.

Donato thought frantically how he could maintain his cover. He realised that the cart's wooden axles were close enough to support him. Lying on his front, with his face in the grit, he put his feet up on the rear axle, then reached up with his hands to grab the front axle, just as the cart started to move. Donato's shoes, which were still a little damp from their dip in the river, accommodated the movement of the rear axle beneath them. Donato had to put his arms round the front axle, with the sleeves of his shirt allowing the axle to turn. He knew he could only hold on a short while in that position before slipping off, and prayed that the cart would get through the gate before he did so.

Finally Donato heard the gate close behind them, and he crumpled thankfully to the ground. Fortunately there was no-one around to see him. He leapt up and ran for the shadows of an overhanging roof at the back of a church. At last, he was in the City – he had achieved his first goal. He had thought that the city of artists would welcome one of its number with open arms. It had not. Donato hoped that life within the City was not going to prove as difficult as getting into the place.

CHAPTER 2

Donato awoke with a start to the clatter of horses' hooves on cobbles. He had been so exhausted after his journey that he had fallen asleep where he sat behind the church. Now, as the first rays of light flicked the ochre roof-tiles high above him, he could see that he was not alone. Rats scampered along the street-side gutters, picking up the scraps of food that lay there, tossed out of people's kitchens straight on to the street for the municipal cleaners to clear away. Although, like his hometown, the City was proud enough to have a troop of sweepers clear away the night's debris in the first hour after dawn every day, the army of paupers and orphans with brooms and carts had not reached him yet.

He kicked an inquisitive rodent away as it sniffed his shoe. *'Don't they know about the plague in this place?'* Donato wondered to himself. Perhaps the City was not such a centre of intellect as he had been led to believe. Most cities had passed a law by now to say that you had to keep your rubbish in your house until you heard the cleaning gang announce its presence on your street with bells or whistles.

Had Florence already forgotten that the population of most of the cities of Italy, and the rest of Europe for that matter, had been halved by the Black Death? Donato had been well schooled in history. On cold winter evenings in their ramshackle little house just outside Lucca, his father would gather the family around a roaring fire and tell them stories of days gone by. Over the years, Donato had learned all about the topsy-turvy fortunes of the cities of Tuscany.

But the plague was more than six generations ago, now just a distant piece of trivia in monks' hand-written history books. Since then, the City he was now in had become one of the richest and most powerful cities in the world, thanks to its trade in wool, silk and other textiles, and through being home to some of the biggest names in banking whose empires had been built on the back of that trade. All the wealth and power must have made the City's leaders complacent.

Donato knew that the biggest name of all had been the Medici family. Their saga was a popular tale to anyone outside Florence – people were always ready to gloat at their downfall. His father had recounted many times how, in the second half of the last century the family expanded from straight-forward banking into virtually ruling the City. The head of the family, Lorenzo *Il Magnifico* had been not only a brilliant leader of the City but also a great patron of the arts and learning. Under him, Florence became the cultural and academic focus of the world in addition to being a commercial centre. Hundreds of families made their fortunes, and spent them on lavish palaces, artistic works and entertainment.

All that changed, though, with Lorenzo's death in 1492. His son Piero *lo Sfortunato*, 'the Unfortunate', had certainly lived up to his nickname. Less astute than his predecessor in many ways - in business, politics and the arts - he only lasted for two years before being driven out of the City. The French were at the time taking over vast swathes of Italy, and occupied Florence for just eight days before doing a deal with the City that enabled their conquering army to continue southwards.

Donato's father delighted in recalling the gruesome story of the 'Mad Monk', Girolamo Savonarola. When the French left, power was seized by Savonarola, a Dominican friar with a prominent nose that accentuated his wild staring eyes to give him the appearance of a demonic eagle. There was ostensibly an elected Council, but Savonarola's hold over the City, established through years of preaching fire and brimstone from his pulpit, was so strong that the Council's primary function was to endorse and then enforce his decisions, much as it had been under the Medici.

Savonarola and his followers reviled the ostentation and debauchery that resulted from the City's affluence, and insisted that its inhabitants return to a life more simple and god-fearing. Initially this was a popular change, but quickly the people tired of having to pile their beautifully crafted books on to specially crafted bonfires, give up their fine clothes and jewellery, and live their lives in fear of being caught at some illicit pleasure.

So Savonarola was burned at the stake, along with two of his fellow monks, in the City's main square, the Piazza della Signoria, for all to see. It had, by all accounts, been a great and well-attended spectacle. In 1498, the democratically elected council, known as the *Signoria*, impotent since the arrival of the Medici, actually took up the role for which it was designed.

Six years later, Florence now seemed to be stable again. The head of the Signoria, *'Gonfaloniere'* Piero Soderini, had been trained in the art of government by Lorenzo the Magnificent, and had proved good at restoring the City's trading links, reputation and pride in itself. That was why Donato had come – to be in a City that was going somewhere, that had a buzz about it, and, above all, that would be able to provide him with the opportunity to become a real artist.

Donato had learned from his father that during the time of Savonarola art had effectively been banned from the City, so the great artists had left for other major states such as Rome, Milan or even France. But with the return of a more liberal regime, many of them had been enticed back – Botticelli, Filippino Lippi, Cronaca and the Sangallo brothers. Also returned was the firebrand from nearby Vinci known simply by his first name, Leonardo, or by the name of the town from which he hailed, as he lacked a surname having been born to the mistress of the town notary.

Donato had walked through Vinci the day before arriving in Florence. The artist was famous throughout Italy for his skills with a paint-brush, but the little town had seemed untouched by the greatness of its illegitimate son – it was no different from any of the other villages that he had passed on his way.

Donato ached to work with one of these giants of

the world of art. Having studied in the workshop of one of Lucca's leading artists, he knew the basics of drawing and painting, and he thought he showed much greater talent than any of the others at the school. He was the brightest of all the pupils academically too, and had been able to learn to read and write, unusual for a young craftsman.

But Lucca was a back-water – to hit the big-time Donato needed to be working with the big names. This would bring him exposure to the richest patrons and enable him to start earning good money for commissions. Then he would be able to travel to all the cities of Italy and lead a life of fame and pleasure.

Donato needed to find his way into a job with a leading artist and work his way up the ladder, and he had a plan of how to do it.

First things first, though. He needed food and water. Water was easy – it flowed plentifully from taps around the City, piped directly via aqueducts from springs in the hills above Florence. Donato did not have any money, so having slaked his thirst from a drinking fountain outside the church, which he found out was dedicated Santa Maria Novella, he stole a strip of dried meat from a market stall. The old stall-owner was engrossed in conversation with his neighbour about some local gossip, and did not even notice Donato slide past and grab it from his counter. He hungrily devoured the leathery meat as soon as he got round the corner.

Feeling rather pleased with himself at the ease of the exercise but still famished, Donato came to a row of bakers' stalls near the solid-looking church of San Lorenzo. He picked up a roll and was just hiding it in his sleeve when the woman who ran the stall, who was as round as an apple, spotted him and gave a shout of alarm. Her husband, curiously as thin as an apple-stalk, picked up a giant rolling pin from behind the counter, and Donato ran to escape. The husband ran after him, and was much faster than Donato. Donato sprinted for all he was worth, knowing that if he was caught, he would certainly be beaten up badly. If he was lucky he might be handed over to the authorities rather than being beaten to death, but that would only result in a further kicking, imprisonment and certain expulsion from the City.

As he ran round a corner, he suddenly came into the Cathedral square, and nearly stopped in awe of the buildings he saw there. But he kept on going. The baker was a couple of arms' lengths from catching him when Donato bounded up the steps of the cathedral to reach its open doors. He ran in, straight across the open floor and out the other side. His pursuer, being a deeply religious man, paused to genuflect and could only walk respectfully across the cathedral's nave – by the time he reached the far door, Donato had disappeared.

With his hunger abated by the bread and meat, Donato spent the rest of the day searching for his target. His plan was to find a palace that was being decorated and that would therefore need some artisans to work on it. He eventually found what he was looking for on Via dei Benci, just before sun-down. It was a brand new palace being built on the site of demolished slums, some of which remained next-door to the building site. So that workmen could lift large items of furniture through the openings, its windows were still without the thick iron bars that adorned those of all the other palaces around the City as a security measure. People were still milling about the City, and Donato elected to return later.

Donato came back to the palace once night had fully fallen. He envisaged getting in through one of the unsecured windows, but, as with all Florentine palaces, they were above head height to prevent prying eyes from peering inside. He took a run at one of the windows from the opposite side of the street, jumped as high as he could and just got his arms over the wide sill of the window. He dragged his body up through the opening and fell heavily on to the stone floor the other side. By the light of the moon and the torches that burned on the wall of the building on the other side of the street, Donato made his way upstairs so that he would hear the workmen coming in the next morning before they saw him. He found a small room, laid down and went to sleep.

In the morning, he woke at first light. His first task was to write up the past couple of days' activities in the leather-bound diary that he had resolved to keep to chart his ventures. There was no sign of any workers, so when he finished writing, Donato walked down the corridor looking into the rooms that led off it. They were all bare – devoid of both furniture and decoration on the walls. The fifth room he came to they had just started to decorate, and all the tools of the trade were in there.

Outside, the massive bell in the Campanile, the bell-tower next to the Cathedral, started to toll. And it did not stop. Donato had lost track of time since leaving Lucca, and now realised that it must be Sunday. The bell was calling the people to church – he would not be disturbed in the palace today. On the seventh day, Italians, like God, rested.

This was just the opportunity that Donato had been hoping for. The men working on the decoration had evidently left in a hurry after their half day's effort on Saturday, probably to hit the wine and the whore-houses the minute the sun set, for he had heard that drink and sex were the two favourite pass-times of the Florentines, in that order. The workers had left a whole covered bucket full of *intonaco*, the fine plaster used as the base for painting frescos, which was still wet. They had also left some rich red, yellow and blue paints, which must have been painstakingly prepared – it could take hours to grind the minerals and plant extracts that made up the finest colours.

The ceiling of the room had already been painted – a sky in the same beautiful deep shade of blue as there had been painted in the sky over Florence all the previous day. At the centre of the ceiling there was depicted a cloud on which sat a woman draped in orange robes, throwing laurel garlands from a basket down to the earth beneath. The walls were bare, as if waiting for Donato to fill them in.

So he started at the top of the wall that bordered the street, first laying the *intonaco* over the layer of deliberately rough plaster left by the builders. Once he had smoothed the *intonaco* with a trowel he started painting, extending the sky a third of the way down the wall until it hit a Roman style villa on a hill, surrounded by cypress trees. The picture expanded around the window to show a Tuscan countryside dotted with Roman buildings, in keeping with the figure on the ceiling.

From his studies, Donato knew that modern

painting invariably followed one of two themes – religious or classical. Donato preferred painting religious scenes (crucifixions were his forte), but he could turn his hand to the more frivolous countryside scenes with ancient Roman or Greek themes that had become fashionable in the last years of the Medici.

He did not have time to make up the preparatory drawings that an artist would usually use when painting a fresco, and there were none lying around from which to take a lead. Whoever was supposed to be painting the room must have taken them away for the weekend. Donato therefore painted freehand, which made the task even harder, especially keeping everything to scale.

He was just finishing the wall as the light started to fade. He had been labouring at a frenetic pace since morning, and as he made his final touches, he realised that he had not eaten all day. He washed out the brushes in a pail of dirty water that was in the room, went downstairs and out through the window he had entered by. No-one noticed him come out – dusk on a Sunday evening was the quietest time in the City. Families would be sitting down for a light supper before having an early night in preparation for the week of work that followed.

Donato walked until he came to a large paved square with a church at the far end. A street sign, something he had never seen before, told him he was in Piazza Santa Croce. There were leather tanning workshops all around the square, interspersed with *trattorias* – eating houses for the workers. Being a Sunday the trattorias were all closed, but as he walked down one side of the square Donato saw that one of them had a stable door the top half of which had been left ajar. There was not a soul about so he pushed it open and jumped through the gap. The moon was already rising brightly directly across the square. Although the window at the front of the room had its shutters drawn, enough light trickled in through the half door-way for Donato to pick his way between the benches and tables to reach the larder at the back.

The only food he could find once he got there was half a dozen eggs. Knowing that the owners of the trattoria probably lived directly above it, he thought better of lighting a fire to cook the eggs. Instead, he cracked them one by one and poured them straight down his throat. Eggs had never been his favourite food, especially when raw, but his hunger and thirst forced him to devour four of them before he could stomach no more.

Donato walked back to the palace, *his* palace for now, climbed through the window again and went to find his sleeping place once more. He wanted to be there when they found his handiwork. He fell into a deep sleep, drained but satisfied from his journey to Florence, his efforts at getting into the City, finding a palace and then his day's work on its walls.

CHAPTER 3

Donato was jolted awake by the pain of a heavy stick being struck repeatedly across his back. His exhaustion had caused him to sleep through dawn and the workmen arriving to start their week. "What the hell are you doing here?" asked a harsh old voice. Donato lifted his head to see a little man with white hair and a long white beard contrasting against a bright red cloak staring malevolently down at him.

The man kept beating Donato with what must have been a walking stick, and shouting abuse. Donato reached his right hand up to catch the stick as another blow rained down on him. He missed it at the first attempt, and he felt a sharp pain in his forearm as the stick struck home. He managed to grab the stick on its next downstroke, and pulled himself up to tower above the old man.

"I needed shelter for the night," Donato explained weakly, his heart thumping hard in his chest.

"Did you paint that rubbish in the room up the

hall-way?" asked the man.

Donato's heart sank. Fully awake now, Donato realised that whoever this was, his cloak and his inimical stick were of high quality so he must be important. It was bad news that his opinion of Donato's painting was "rubbish". Donato guessed he must have been the owner of the palace. "Yes, I wanted to show what I could do so that you might employ me, but if it's not what you wanted I'll take the plaster off and start again. I deduced from the ceiling that you wanted a Roman theme, so…"

"How dare you come into my house and guess what I want on my walls" the old man interrupted. "You're damned right that you'll take the plaster off. Then you'll re-apply it and let my painters paint a proper picture, and you'll do it fast or I'll call the Guard and have you thrown in *Le Stinche*."

Donato had heard of the notorious Florentine prison known as *Le Stinche* even in Lucca. Florence was unusual in having a prison – punishments in Lucca, like most other places, took the form of public beatings, exile or death, depending on the severity of the crime. Rumour had it that conditions in *Le Stinche* were dire, and that death was preferable to even the briefest stay in there.

Only the previous evening, while on his search for food, Donato had walked passed a forbidding stone cube of a building, from which he had heard moans of anguish rising through the few ventilation holes in the wall. He assumed that this was the place, and had no desire to find out how terrible it was from the inside.

"Ok, but please let me do some of the painting. I'll paint anything you want. If you don't like it I'll tear it down again, but please give me this chance. I'll prove to you that I'm a good artist. I'll work for nothing if you want." Now that the old man's anger had subsided a little, Donato thought he had a chance to win him over. The man grabbed Donato's arm with a surprisingly vice-like grip, and marched him down the hall to the room where Donato had spent the previous day hard at work.

The room was now being decorated at full tilt. Labourers were throwing plaster up on to the other three walls. In the middle of the room a tall skinny man with long greasy hair looked up from a set of designs laid out on a trestle table that had been set up to tell a young boy, who could have been no older than twelve, what paints would need to be made up for the day. Donato presumed this must be the artist who had been commissioned to decorate the palace.

The artist greeted the old man reverentially. "Good morning Messer Corsini. Have you been in over the weekend? It seems we have lost some of our paints and they've been replaced by this picture" he said, gesturing at Donato's scene. "It's rather good I think." The old man assumed that the artist was attempting to flatter his employer with his compliment for the painting, just in case it had been the palace's owner who had done the decoration – it was well known that he was a keen, but mediocre, artist.

"Of course I haven't been in, and if I had, do you think I'd have done something like this, when we've agreed that you would paint this room to be the inside of a Greek temple? It was this idiot. I found him asleep in one of the rooms. He's going to make up for it by taking the plaster off and helping you put that temple up."

Donato did not utter a word, lest the old man should change his mind about allowing him to help repaint the wall. He was happy to spend the rest of the day working alongside the labourers and assistants. He did not mind hacking off the plaster that bore his painting, as he knew that he at least had the opportunity to show the chief artist that he was worth employing. He was even happier to be invited to share the workers' lunch of bread, hard ewe's milk cheese and wine.

As the light faded and they began to pack up for the evening, Donato asked the artist, who he found out over lunch was a wool-trader called Giovanni Anziani, whether he could come back tomorrow. Anziani had not spoken to Donato all day other than to bark instructions at him, but now Donato was shocked to hear Anziani invite him back to his own home. "Your painting was good, very good considering that you must have been painting freehand – where did you learn?"

"I taught myself, studying the pictures in the churches of Lucca and Pisa. I have also been to art school a little. Do you mean I can carry on painting here?"

"Yes, unlike the old man, I can see that you have potential. And I can smell that you have nowhere to wash and sleep. You've worked hard today to right your wrongs. I can't pay you anything, but you can stay with me until we finish Corsini's place. We'll see whether you can work hard enough to make it in this game. It's not just a question of talent – you've got to have backbone too."

* * * * *

Giovanni Anziani lived in a small house on the other side of the river, a short walk from the Ponte Carraia near the small (for Florence) church of *San Frediano in Cestello*. It was a clean and simple house, one up, one down. The upper level was accessed via a wooden ladder. Up there slept Anziani and his wife Grazia who, following a glowing introduction from her husband, gave Donato a warm welcome into their home.

Their son Giovannino would have shared the room with them had he not been stillborn eighteen years previously. Grazia had been unable to conceive further children following that trauma, but Giovanni counted himself lucky that she had survived the birth, unlike the wives of many men he knew who had suffered similar experiences.

Downstairs there was a fire-place and some chairs around a large oak table. After a peasant dinner of *ribollita*, a thick vegetable and bean soup on top of stale bread, Grazia found some old blankets for Donato to sleep between on the floor downstairs. Donato appreciated going to sleep with a full belly and some covers. Apart from the battering he'd taken that morning, from which he was still sore, Donato reflected that things were going well, and he drifted contentedly off to sleep.

For the next week, Donato worked as hard as he could. At the end of each day, he dined with Anziani and his wife. She spoke very little, never having truly recovered from the loss of her child. After dinner, while Grazia insisted on clearing up alone, Donato dutifully wrote by candle-light in his diary before going to sleep.

Anziani was pleased to have someone to talk to over dinner, and Donato was keen to hear as much as he could about the artistic community of Florence. The City was winning back its artistic spirit after the wilderness years of Savonarola. Commissions for public works were being issued now that art and adornment was acceptable again. Leonardo from Vinci was the big cheese once more, as he had been before Savonarola, but there was a young pretender to his throne, called Michelangelo Buonarroti.

It would be interesting, according the Anziani, to see whether Buonarroti would take Leonardo's artistic crown. Buonarroti was a sculptor whereas Leonardo was primarily a painter. Buonarroti was a hard and diligent worker, while Leonardo flitted from project to project, often moving on to the next before finishing the last. Leonardo was a society character, in contrast with his competitor who was socially inept. Leonardo was rich, with forty years of well-paid commissions behind him, even though many of his patrons came after him for the return of their advance payments when their assignments were not seen through to completion.

Long before the Medici had been ousted from Florence, Leonardo had migrated to Milan and made his fortune. Buonarroti had yet to establish his name in Florence when the Medici fell – he left for Rome, but with no reputation to precede him, it was harder to win good work. Both artists had been born in villages just outside Florence – Vinci to the West and Caprese to the East, but they were Florentines through and through. Their rivalry was developing nicely thought Anziani.

By day, Anziani was impressed with Donato's

effort and skill, and when Corsini came for his regular inspection at the end of the week, Anziani told him as much. Donato was up at first light every morning, keen to get to the palace to start work – he had often left the house before Anziani was dressed. And the lad was always the last to leave as the sun set.

Even with Lodovico Corsini's limited artistic abilities, he could tell that Donato was good. Anziani was a good but unambitious artist, and Corsini was satisfied with his reports of Donato's hard work – with both talent and dedication the boy might go far. He could perhaps even become one of the leading artists of the City.

Corsini figured that he could, if he was careful, foster Donato and bathe in the glory that would come if he fulfilled that potential. He would have to give Donato the chance to make a reputation for himself, yet not give him so much independence that Donato could blossom without Corsini's influence and assistance. Whenever he brought members of Florentine society to inspect the progress of work at the palace, as he often did to show off the ripening fruits of his considerable investment, he made a point of drawing their attention to the work of his new protégé, only telling them that it was by a young artist he had discovered but without revealing his name. He told Anziani to keep pushing, but also to provide as much guidance as he could.

Three weeks later, the decoration of the rooms on the first floor of the palace was complete. Anziani's reports on Donato, and what he had seen of the boy's talents with his own eyes, had been so positive that Corsini calculated that it was time to show his discovery off to Florentine society, before anybody else could interfere. On his next

Friday afternoon visit, therefore, he invited Donato to his current palace for dinner the following night.

Corsini also wanted Donato to look the part for the dinner. He brought a fine blue silk shirt and hose to wear, and gave him a few coins to go and get a shave and a hair-cut before the dinner, recommending his own long-standing barber Nello. His final gift was a solid gold lion-shaped brooch, which he removed from his own chest and pinned on Donato in gratitude for his work.

"I have taken you at your word, and not paid you anything for your efforts, but you have done well. Please look after this brooch – it is a valuable symbol of Florence. But keep it well hidden and do not wear it about, as there are many violent types in this City who would rob you in an instant. They would not dare to assault me for it, but they would have no qualms about knocking you out for a quick profit."

CHAPTER 4

As Donato, still in shock at Corsini's generosity, was arriving for dinner in his fine new clothes at the old merchant's current palace, half a mile away and on the other side of the river, a shadowy figure climbed over a wall in the evening twilight to land in the garden of the Pitti family's palace. Carrying two leather bags, joined by a leather yolk slung over his shoulder, he crept into the palace unseen and, following instructions that he had memorised, found the gallery.

He was only able to pick up two items from those on display before one of the palace's servants walked in on him placing the second, a solid gold plate, three hand spans across and encrusted with emeralds, sapphires and rubies the size of coins, in the bag. The servant shouted to raise the alarm, then moved to stop the thief. The thief took the bag off his shoulder and swung one end with both hands and considerable difficulty at the approaching servant's head.

Unfortunately for the servant, that half of the bag already contained the first item that the thief had taken, an ancient Roman marble bust of Julius Caesar. It connected with its target with a dull thud and the servant crumpled to the ground. The thief knew instantly that the mass of marble in his bag had killed the man stone dead. Rather than try to pick up anything else to put in his bag, which was already straining with the weight inside it and was almost too heavy to carry, he decided to make a run for it before further interference.

He burst out of the doors into the garden at the back of the palace, just as two servants who had heard the commotion entered the room. They gave chase and, with the heavy bag over the thief's shoulder slowing him down, they were gaining on him. The thief came to the ladder that he had found on his way in and placed against the wall just for this purpose. He started to climb the ladder up the twelve foot high wall, his calf and thigh muscles burning with the effort of lifting the extra weight of his bounty.

The servants were closing in on the ladder as he neared its summit. As the first of them started to climb, the thief stepped off on to the top of the wall. It was barely a foot wide, and he had to balance carefully as he lifted the top of the ladder away from the wall. The extra ballast of the bag on one shoulder allowed him to push the ladder out with the opposite arm. The servant, who was by now halfway up, had no choice but to jump off as the ladder fell backwards.

It was a ten-foot drop the other side of the wall, and he knew that if he jumped now, with the weight in his bag, either the marble would smash on the cobbles of the street below or he would break his leg. However, the ground over which the street ran rose further along the wall. The thief walked carefully along the top of the wall until the ground on the other side was high enough for him to jump down more safely. As he left the wall he could see a dozen or more servants running across the grounds to catch him. The next servant on the scene had repositioned the ladder and was now nearing the top of the wall, and more were following him up.

As planned, his twelve year-old brother was waiting for him a little further up the street, standing by a horse. The thief put the bag down, scrambled into the saddle and waited for his brother to pass him the bag. But the boy could not lift it. "Come on, *figlio di puttana*", the thief screamed, as two servants jumped from the wall only yards from where they were. They both stumbled when they landed on the cobbles, their flat-soled slippers being designed for carrying out their duties around the palace with the minimum of noise rather than for giving chase to intruders.

The boy managed to get the bag a few inches off the ground, just enough for his sibling to reach down from his mount and grab the strap. He pulled the bag up with a mighty effort, and was seriously entertaining the thought of leaving the boy there. But the knowledge that his little brother would most likely be beaten to death made him think again. He reached his other arm down and pulled the boy up on to the horse – one advantage of under-nourishment was that he was as light as a feather - then gave the horse a vicious dig in the ribs and they were off in the instant that the servants were upon them.

"That was too close Marco" said the younger of the two, who knew that his life had been saved by a whisker, as the street petered out into a donkey track. The mangy horse tired quickly under the weight of two people and their bounty trying to tear up the hill towards the church of San Miniato al Monte. "Well if you'd stayed on the horse like we planned, it would have been much easier, you idiot. I don't want to hear another word from you until we get there," shouted Marco over his shoulder.

The brothers knew that a family as powerful as the Pitti would be able to launch a large search party of militia, so they had to get to safety quickly. Luckily safety was not far off. It came in the shape of the church that lay ahead of them at the top of the hill. It was the Prior of San Miniato church and monastery who had offered to pay Marco and his brother Silvio twenty florins to carry out the theft. The brothers had no idea why the Prior should want to do such a thing, but it was a princely sum that they could not turn down.

Marco could not be sure that he had the right piece of marble. There had been six in the room, and they all looked similar. He had picked the one with the laurels around its head on the assumption that this was most likely to be Julius Caesar. The Prior had given clear directions to the room, and had been specific that it must be Julius Caesar that Marco came away with, nothing else would do. He had not told Marco that there would be a selection to choose from.

Marco and Silvio were an accomplished yet innocent-looking team, which was why the Prior had come to them for his dirty work. Even had they known of the plate, they would not have dreamt of stealing it normally, as there was no way they would be able to get rid of such a conspicuous item. The Prior had told Marco that the plate would be on display in the same room as the marble bust and would be an easy target. He had also said that there were many other treasures in the same room, and promised an extra few florins if they could come away with one of the other valuable antiquities on display.

When they reached his church, the thieves did not have time to admire the extraordinary views that it offered over the City, and went straight round to the rear. There would be no-one around at this time on a Saturday evening except, they hoped, the Prior himself. They had to clamber over a large pile of rubble, which had been the church's bell-tower until its destruction by a mild earthquake a few years previously, to reach the sacristy door. They knocked loudly, and heard the Prior's footsteps cracking over the flagstones of the church floor towards them. He unlocked the door and let the two youngsters in. He told them to hide the bag under the main altar, and then to go and pray for forgiveness in the crypt beneath the choir-stalls.

The light had by now all but faded, and the inside of the church, lit with candles, was an inviting sanctuary. They did as they were told. Meanwhile the Prior took the saddle off the horse and gave the animal a whack on the backside, unworried about whether he would see it again. The horse bolted on up the hill.

Marco and Silvio had only been praying for a short while when two militia-men, one holding a large flaming torch, came in through the church's main door, which was always open. On seeing the priest, one of them said "Prior, we are looking for two thieves who came this way – have you seen anyone looking suspicious this evening?"

"No," replied the priest, "except you". Marco and Silvio could hear the exchange echoing through the church. They silently thanked the God in whose house they were kneeling for the fact that, even though he was a fat and lascivious looking man, the soldiers would not dare to doubt a priest. "But you are welcome to come in and search the place," the prior bluffed.

"Very well, in order to confirm to our master that we have performed our task properly, we will look around." The priest had not expected such conscientiousness – militia-men were usually the epitome of laziness unless in battle, and sometimes even then too. The young thieves' hearts beat faster and faster as they heard the soldiers' heavy footsteps getting nearer and nearer to the stairs down to the crypt.

They heard the pace of the steps slow as the men engaged the church's steps. The boys huddled together terrified – the walls in the crypt were solid and there was nowhere to go. But the sound of the footsteps passed overhead and they realised with relief that the men had gone up the central steps that led to the altar. When they reached it, the steps stopped, before turning round and coming back down the stairs and continuing back through the nave.

The two were evidently just going through the motions of performing a search, and were not interested in searching any of the rooms off the nave, such as the sacristy, vestry, chapels or crypt. Eventually the footsteps became quieter as the men returned to the church's entrance, and then left without any further word being spoken.

Part of the deal that the thieves had struck with the Prior was that he would give them shelter for the night. The wall that Marco had climbed over, as well as being the wall to the Pitti's garden, formed part of the City wall, and the hill on which San Miniato stood therefore lay outside the City boundary. There was no way that they would be able to get back into the City this evening. The Prior led them back into the Sacristy and told them they could sleep on the wooden benches, but that they had to be out at first light before the Dominican monks whose monastery was attached to the church came in for their early morning prayer.

The Prior fetched the bag from under the altar, only just able to lift it. He took out the golden platter and regarded it jealously before putting it back in the bag, but showed no interest in the older, less glistening, object. He then carried the bag to the Bishop's Palace, which also adjoined the Church. The Bishop of Florence only came here in July and August, to escape the searing heat in the City. As Florence was enclosed by hills all around, the heat and stillness of summer made it unbearable, and had earned the City the nick-name *La Padella*, or 'frying pan'. Although the Palace was only a mile or so from the centre, it was far enough up the hill to receive a light cooling breeze.

For the rest of the year, the Palace lay empty. The Prior held keys to the palace but was not supposed to enter it without the Bishop's say-so. Tonight, however, he knew this was the safest place to hide the stolen goods. He did not let his accomplices in there, knowing that the few treasures that were in the palace would be gone by the morning were he to do so.

He put the bag in the Bishop's bedroom. At the end of the week, he would retrieve it to give to the man who had promised to rebuild his bell-tower in return for the Prior arranging the theft. Like Marco, the Prior had no idea why the man wanted these particular items so badly.

CHAPTER 5

Donato sat down to dinner, stunned by the company he found himself in. He had not had any idea how important Corsini was until this moment. The banqueting table was laid for sixty people. The few of them that Donato had been introduced to so far were the political, artistic and society names that Donato had heard Anziani gossip about as they sat in his house after dinner. He now found himself sitting between Gonfaloniere Piero Soderini, leader of the City's government, and Giuliano da Sangallo, one of the leading artists of the generation.

Corsini went out of his way to make sure that his guests enjoyed themselves. In the corner, a group of musicians playing lutes, a pipe and drums accompanied a eunuch singing verses from the Divine Comedy. The wine flowed, and a jester walked among the company doing tricks.

The host anticipated that Donato would lack the social skills to mix at this level, which was why he had placed him next to the consummate politician Soderini, who had the gift of being able to talk to anyone at their own level, and the garrulous Sangallo, who could talk the hind legs off a donkey.

Earlier in the evening, before the guests sat for dinner, Corsini had introduced Donato to Gonfaloniere Soderini as the next big Florentine artist. Donato had mumbled that he was sure he could never compete with Leonardo, but Soderini smoothly replied that if Messer Corsini said he was the next big thing then that is what he would be. Now, at the dinner table, Soderini pointed out to Donato the leading figures of Florentine society. Donato could not believe how quickly things were moving for him.

Along with Soderini's brother, Cardinal Francesco Soderini, the heads of all the great dynasties were there – the Pazzi, the Strozzi, the Albizzi, the Pitti and the many other great Florentine merchant and banking houses. There was Agostino Vespucci, an ambitious young politician whose family's wealth and fame had soared since his older cousin Amerigo had set sail in search of westward routes to the spices of the East Indies and accidentally landed on a whole new continent.

Federico Benvenuti was there too. He was reputedly the richest man in Florence, yet people knew very little about him. New money was also present in the form of Gianluca Galeazzo, a cloth-merchant from Milan. Soderini did not hesitate to explain his family background to Donato, with unusual distaste.

"Galeazzo is the bastard son of Galeazzo Maria Sforza, the fifth Duke of Milan. It seems he was disowned by the Duke without a ducat to his name, for what reason I have never discovered. He used his name to make a fortune through trade and, unfortunately, settled here in Florence. Despite his mercantile skills, Galeazzo portrays himself as a deeply religious man, and was one of Savonarola's disciples. I think that his show of piety is just a front to garner people's trust. You would do well to steer clear of him."

In addition to Sangallo, the artistic community was represented by Leonardo, the aging Filippino Lippi and Michelangelo Buonarroti, who, Soderini told Donato, was nearing completion of the greatest statue since Roman times. The Gonfaloniere knew this, because he himself had commissioned the statue on behalf of the people – it would be a grand statement about the strength of Florence despite the City's relatively small size.

There lay on the table a vast array of golden cutlery and fine china. Everyone used a pronged instrument that Donato had never seen before to eat with, which his neighbour informed him was called a *'forchetta'*. The food was almost all new to Donato, apart from the familiar wild boar, of which there was a whole roast in the centre of the display. In a demonstration of wealth, many of the other foods were spiced with rare ingredients from the orient such as cloves and saffron.

There were sweetbreads, quails' eggs, roasted peacocks (with their tail-feathers reinstated once out of the oven) and pies stuffed with live blackbirds which fluttered around the room once the crust was broken. There were also foods that were new to many of the other guests – potatoes and what appeared to be rat-like creatures that had been brought back from Amerigo Vespucci's travels. There followed sugared almonds and candied fruits. Donato was unused to such rich foods, and could not manage any of the more traditional cheeses, which he favoured, served at the end of the meal.

During the feast, he observed what Anziani meant about the differences between Leonardo and Michelangelo – Leonardo was the centre of attention among his surrounding diners, who seemed either to be charmed by the tales he was telling or to be paying him full attention out of sycophancy. The younger artist in contrast sat sullenly at one end of the table, speaking when spoken to, but not engaging anyone freely. He scowled at servants as they tried to serve him.

Donato was intrigued by both men. What a diary entry tonight would make! As the food was being removed, he asked Soderini whether he could make an introduction to either of them.

Soderini was about to reply when there was a commotion outside the door by which they were seated. A pair of servants were demanding to see Messer Pitti, but were being refused entry by Corsini's own staff. Corsini's chamberlain went to speak to the servants to avert an embarrassing scene, and reported to his master that there had been a burglary at the Palazzo Pitti that they wanted to report to Messer Pitti. Corsini found Pitti and passed the message on discretely.

Pitti went to speak to his servants in the doorway. Donato could see by his angry reaction to the news he was being given that it was not good. As Pitti's voice rose, Donato gathered that some valuable treasure had been stolen from his palace. There seemed little that Pitti could do – according to the servants, his son Buonaccorso had reported the theft to the City police – but he made his apologies to Corsini and left. He walked with the servants back to his palace to take stock of his losses.

Pitti was not an overly materialistic man. His enormous wealth had been inherited rather than earned. However, like most Florentines, he was extremely proud of his family's name and achievements. Those achievements included assembling one of the finest collections of artefacts in the City. Now he was being told that his two most prized objects had been taken. Pitti was not as concerned about the death of one of his servants. He had plenty of those, but the stolen items were unique.

The plate had been made by the artist and goldsmith Lorenzo Ghiberti for Cosimo Medici, grandfather of Lorenzo il Magnifico. Cosimo was one of the founding fathers of the Medici dynasty, still revered in Florence as *Pater Patriae*, the Father of the State. He had developed the Medici family bank to be the richest bank in Europe. Florence was a republic, and was proud of its government elected from the merchants' guilds, but Cosimo's financial power allowed him to wield enormous political influence. He was also the first great patron of the arts, commissioning pieces both for his own palace and as public works for the City, the latter being part of his astute manoeuvring to consolidate his popularity and power. The plate was one of the most valuable items in Florence – it weighed twenty pounds exactly.

Cosimo Medici had also been fascinated with the Ancient worlds of Greece and Rome. He started the family collection of classical statues and also its interest in ancient literature and philosophy. Now, forty years after his death, Florentines were almost ruled by the writings of Ancient Rome – barely a single policy or decision could be reached without reference to historical precedent recorded by the likes of Cicero and Livy. The bust, said to have been carved the year before Caesar's death, was beyond price.

The Pitti were a powerful family, even more so now that the Medici had been ejected from their seat of power on the Via Larga. Both of the stolen items had come to the family after the redistribution (or, more accurately, looting) of the Medici's treasures which followed that eviction. Pitti's father had paid out handsomely to track the items down and secure them for his own collection, purely as a way of establishing his family's superiority over the ousted Medici.

Pitti swore he would find who was responsible for the theft and wreak his revenge. He knew that a common thief would not have gone out of his way to select those two pieces from the hundreds that were on display in the palace – it had to be someone who knew his onions from his shallots, a nobleman (which seemed to Pitti to be a contradictory epithet – a noble man would not steal like this).

His first thought was that it must be the Medici themselves, trying to prise back some assets from their exile in Rome. Lorenzo il Magnifico's fat lazy son Giovanni had been manoeuvred into a Cardinal's hat at the age of just thirteen, and the family were beginning to build a power base in the Eternal City. Were they planning a return to the seat of their former power? That would be bad news for the Pitti and the other big Florentine families whose fortunes were now booming. The Medici would be bound to want to settle a few old scores arising from their banishment. Pitti resolved to discuss his concerns with his old friend Gonfaloniere Soderini.

CHAPTER 6

The two brothers set out from San Miniato church early the next morning, as commanded by the Prior. They had another job to do for him, this time much more dangerous. They knew that if they got caught they would almost certainly be executed in some fashion, such as being hanged from the parapet of the Palazzo della Signoria for the amusement of the public.

Marco and Silvio scrambled back down the hill they had torn up the previous day, avoiding the track this time. At the bottom, the City gates had not yet been opened, so they skirted along the wall towards the river to a small but well-known hole in the wall, and passed through. They took the first opportunity to cross the river, over the Ponte Alle Grazie, into the city centre and away from the Palazzo Pitti.

They walked innocently past the Palazzo della Signoria, knowing they would return there shortly to do their work. When they reached the *Mercato Vecchio*, the old market place, they stopped to celebrate their good fortune with a sumptuous breakfast of dried figs and apricots and fresh pastries, washed down with goats milk. They paid with some of the money that the Prior had advanced them to bribe their way into the Signoria palace.

Having taken their fill they retraced their steps to the government palace. They passed over the point where, six years previously, Savonarola and two of his monks had been hanged and burnt. They skirted the statue of the Marzocco lion, one of the many symbols of Florence, at the Northern corner of the palace, came to the entrance to the Palazzo opposite the Palazzo della Mercatanzia and knocked quietly. There was no response so they knocked more loudly. This time a guard came to the door.

"We have an urgent message for Gonfaloniere Soderini from the Duke of Ferrara" said Marco.

"The hell you do," responded the guard, eying them contemptuously in their rags. While the boys who stood before him were dishevelled enough to have just ridden from Ferrara, he thought a man such as that would never have sent two young boys with an urgent message.

Silvio brought out a purse, which bore the emblem of the Duke of Ferrara. The Prior of San Miniato, who had been given the purse by the Duke himself on a previous visit to Florence, had handed it to them two days ago with the money in. "Here are twenty florins that say we do." Actually there were only nineteen, as they had just used one from the purse to buy breakfast. With the change, they had left a handsome tip for the pretty young girl that had served them, and they still now had a few small coins left over. But Marco knew the guard would not want to spend time counting the coins until he reached the safety of his own quarters later in the day.

Twenty florins was about half a year's salary for the guard, and the purse with the Duke's coat of arms completed the trick of persuading him that he ought to let them in whatever his doubts as to their authenticity. It was widely known that a delegation from Ferrara was due to arrive in Florence, so it was just conceivable that these two bore an advance message from the Duke.

He gave them a cursory frisk to ensure that they had no weapons concealed in their clothes. He did not want to delay too long in case a colleague arrived, in which case he would have to explain why he was letting two youths in so easily, and would either have to share his prize or, worse, have to give it up altogether, lose his job and probably either his freedom or his life too. He did not detect the lumps of charcoal that the boys had hidden in their undergarments.

As it was still early that Saturday morning, the full retinue of the palace had not yet sprung into action. Having got past the sentinel at the doorway, Marco and Silvio were able to follow the directions that the Prior had given them, through the courtyard of thick columns, and up the stairs. When they reached the top, they turned into the *Salone dei Cinquecento*, the grand Hall of Five Hundred, that Savonarola had had built shortly before his death by Il Cronaca to house the enlarged government that he had installed in the City.

The room was now a symbol of democracy, as Savonarola had replaced Medici rule over Florence with an elected parliament which, since his death, was flourishing.

On a number of occasions the Medici had tried to regain power, and the boys could only suspect that the instructions for this latest job had come directly from the Medici camp. Only they would want to make such a statement against democracy, as they had been the biggest losers as a result of it.

Marco and Silvio put the large timber beam that leant against the wall across its brackets on the door, locking it in case they were disturbed. The room could only be locked from the inside so that Council sessions could not be disturbed. Pulling the charcoal out of their pants, they set about their task. The palace staff had been decorating the room all that week in readiness for the Duke's visit, and there was nothing further for them to do until the party arrived from the North. This was lucky for the two thieves, as it meant that no-one needed to enter the room while they were there.

They finished their work quickly and left, able to sneak out through the palace kitchens which were now a hive of activity. They ran past the lions that were kept in a large cage on Via dei Leoni, which had been a feature of Florence for hundreds of years, and returned to the market in high spirit, to seek out the girl who had served them breakfast. Rarely had they enjoyed their profession as criminals for hire so much as today. They knew that in a short while, a scandal would break that would embarrass the City and spread like wild-fire. They were only sorry that they would not be able to bask in the glory of having been its perpetrators.

CHAPTER 7

Gonfaloniere Soderini opened the doors to the Salone dei Cinquecento with pride. Ercole d'Este, the ageing Duke of Ferrara had last visited Florence in the days of the Medici, when the palace's grand hall was only big enough for two hundred. Although Soderini, along with the rest of the City, felt that Savonarola had become power-hungry and self-obsessed to the point of madness in his final months, he recognised the enlargement of the main state room as one of the many benefits that the friar had brought to the City.

Soderini's face dropped as he entered the hall, followed by the Duke and his advisors, as well as Soderini's own intimate counsellors. Across the entire expanse of the room's walls there were charcoal *graffiato* drawings of sexual organs up to head height (the boys were, like most Florentines outside the nobility and clergy, illiterate and so could not write the anti-republic slogans that the Prior had at first requested). The Gonfaloniere was normally so composed, with wise words for every occasion, but the acute embarrassment that this caused, not just to him personally but to his whole beloved City, left him speechless.

One of the Gonfaloniere's deputies, the quick-witted second chancellor Niccolò Machiavelli, took the situation under control. "My Lords, it appears that a clown has obtained access to the Hall and thought we may appreciate some artwork on our plain walls. I can only apologise and ask you to follow me to the Sala dei Gigli where we will hold our Court instead. I will arrange for the perpetrators of this foul insult to be caught and executed."

Grateful for Machiavelli's intervention, which gave him time to recover a little, Soderini led the party up the stairs to the substitute hall. The smaller Sala dei Gigli was always held ready for conferences even though the Salone dei Cinquecento was now preferred. Soderini walked slowly and silently, his face ashen, feeling sick with shame. He knew that the Duke of Ferrara, who was presently not on the friendliest of terms with Florence, would not keep this to himself. The City would be the laughing stock of Europe within weeks. Soderini, as Gonfaloniere, elected for life only 2 years previously to the role that brought residential apartments in the palace itself, would shoulder much of the blame and would be the butt of countless jibes and jokes for years to come.

Florence at this time held a delicate position in Europe. The Medici had lifted the City to a position of commercial and cultural pre-eminence. Savonarola had reversed that progress. Under his regime the trappings of commercial success were to be frowned upon. Hundreds of works of art as well as books, both handwritten and a few of the very first printed versions, were burnt in the Piazza della Signoria on his *Falò delle Vanità*, the 'Bonfires of the Vanities'. On exactly the same spot, Savonarola later met his own fiery end, burned at the stake with two of his followers when the majority of the City's population eventually tired of his imposition of austerity.

Machiavelli summoned the captain of the Palace Guard and questioned him as to how anyone could have got in to do this. Captain Scalieri was a weather-beaten man in his mid-forties with a gruff voice and a slight limp, from a leg injury that he had sustained in a battle to the north of Florence during the French invasion ten years previously.

"Sir, Saturday is not a day on which the Council sits, so all entrances would have been locked from the inside this morning. Therefore whoever did this is either a member of the palace staff or has persuaded someone on the inside to let them in. I will conduct immediate enquiries."

"See that you do," replied Machiavelli. "I do not need to tell you what embarrassment these criminals have caused to the Signoria and to the City, and how important it is that they should be caught immediately. The party from Ferrara must see justice dispensed upon them before they leave the City."

The captain knew this meant execution, which heightened his appetite to find the wrong-doers. His sadistic side even hoped that the old tradition of throwing criminals to the lions that still lived in the cage on Via dei Leoni (but were now fed on the finest cuts of beef) might be revived to create a special impression. The Captain had a reputation for ruthlessness, which he enjoyed and took every opportunity to enhance.

Scalieri ordered every external door to the Palazzo to be locked, then all members of the Guard to assemble in the *Cortile della Dogana*, the Customs Courtyard, immediately beneath the Salone dei Cinquecento, into which Silvio and Marco had first come when let into the Palazzo. The shrewd captain knew that none of the palace staff would be stupid enough to risk certain death by committing such a reckless act themselves, but a guard might just have been fooled into letting somebody into the palace. Although he wanted to catch the criminals quickly, he knew he had to root out the insider first, otherwise he risked sending out a bad hawk that would not return with its prey.

He paced up and down the three lines of guards who now stood crisply to attention. His limp created an uneven rhythm on the flagstones that echoed off the cold walls and through the silence of his men, as he penetratingly inspected each face for signs of guilt. Word had already spread throughout the Palazzo of the intruders' actions, and the guards were itching for a bit of action.

"All guards on door duty this morning step forward" Scalieri commanded. Twelve guards took one step forward. He figured that, whether the entry was pre-arranged or gained on the spur of the moment, it could only have taken place with the connivance of one of these men. Scalieri ordered the twelve into the *Camera delle Arme*, the weapons room, and proceeded to inspect them, again in total silence except for his stilted steps, hoping to unnerve the rogue in their midst.

Scalieri had deliberately taken them into weapons

room, in the hope that the culprit might panic and pick up one of the arms to fight his way out, but no-one gave himself away. The Captain did, however, notice an incongruous bulge in the hose of one of the guards as he completed his inspection. Was the man unusually excited at the thought of action, or was there something else?

"I need to find the most athletic amongst you, so that we can catch these criminals, as they will be making their escape quickly. The three of you who can jump the highest I will send along the route they were spotted leaving by. Jump!"

The guards jumped up in unison. As they landed, Scalieri heard the jingle of coins, and noticed that the bulge that he had spotted had dropped a couple of inches down one leg of the guard's hose. Scalieri summoned that guard and two others forward. There were groans from the others, who all felt that they had jumped the highest and should therefore be given the honour of having the best opportunity to chase these traitors down, but they were ordered to return to the waiting parade lines in the Cortile della Dogana.

"Does anyone have anything to declare?" Scalieri asked of the remaining three men. Silence. He stared intently at each guard in turn, and suddenly lashed out with his fist at the man with the bulge. The guard was hit in the stomach, and fell to the floor, winded. While the two other guards watched incredulously, Scalieri reached inside the man's hose, and pulled out a purse. They saw that it had the Duke of Ferrara's emblem on it, and were even more astonished when Scalieri tipped it up for a handful of gold coins to come cascading out.

"So, Tedesco, you are the Judas who betrayed the honour of the guard and of Florence." Scalieri pulled the errant guard by the hair over to what looked like a scaffold in the corner of room. The Camera delle Arme not only contained weapons for the defence of the Palazzo, but it also housed the sinister machinery used to extract information during interrogations. The most effective in the collection was the *Strappado*, and Scalieri licked his lips at the thought of putting it into action.

The Captain ordered the two innocent guards to tie their colleague's hands together behind his back and on to the hook which hung down from the apex of a tall wooden frame on a twelve foot length of rope. They executed his order with relish, happy to play whatever part they could in avenging the damage done to the City of which they were so proud. The guards were salivating at the prospect of what they knew was to come, joyous that they were the two fortunate enough to have been chosen to see it.

Scalieri turned a winch to hoist the rope. As Tedesco's weight slowly left the floor, borne by his arms behind him, his body tipped forward and he winced as his shoulders took the load.

Scalieri carried on winding until the captive was six feet off the floor. Tedesco grimaced in pain, but he was determined to make no noise. The Captain then released the rope so that the prisoner dropped a couple of feet before the teeth on the winch locked the rope once more. He screamed in agony as his shoulders jarred and strained to leave their sockets. Scalieri asked no questions though, and instead repeated the process twice. Each time the pain and the screams grew. Scalieri usually liked to take things more slowly with the Strappado, leaving the prisoner suspended for at least an hour before starting the drops, but today he needed information quickly.

The prisoner now screamed for mercy, at which Scalieri asked him who he had let into the Palazzo that morning. Tedesco said that it had been two young men who claimed to be messengers of the Duke of Ferrara with an important message for Gonfaloniere Soderini. At this, Scalieri, winched Tedesco up for another drop, for the sheer stupidity of letting them in on the basis that they offered him gold and without calling any of his colleagues to assist in the verification of their identities.

Scalieri dropped Tedesco for the fourth time, and kept him bound to the machine while he extracted a detailed description of the two youths. When he had as much information as he was going to get, he hauled Tedesco back up for a final time, and stormed out to the Courtyard to brief the rest of the guard on who they were looking for. Tedesco would be left to stew up there and, eventually, die.

Scalieri despatched sixteen of his guards to search the City for the intruders, with instructions to bring them back alive but to use whatever force was necessary to apprehend them, no matter how young they seemed. They fanned out from the Palazzo in troops of four – to the north towards the cathedral, east to Santa Croce, south for the river and west across the Piazza della Signoria in the direction of the markets. They had descriptions of their targets' approximate ages, hair and what they were wearing.

It was not long before the group that was searching to the West came to the *Mercato Nuovo*, the new market that sold silks, wools and other textiles. After searching the stalls and shops around the small market square they went north up the Via Calimala to the Mercato Vecchio. The older market was a bustling array of stalls selling the produce of the farmers, bakers, pastry-makers, vineyard-owners, beekeepers and scavengers of Florence and its environs. Around the edge of the market there were stalls of moneylenders interspersed with little hospitality stalls that served milk, wine and pastries. Customers could sit on small *banchi*, or benches, outside, which were mostly left by unsuccessful moneylenders who had gone out of business, and which had given their name to the grander banks now operated from within palaces by the more successful families.

Marco and Silvio were sitting at one of the banchi, chatting to the girl who had served them earlier. Marco, who was not totally at ease, spotted the troop of guards searching in the middle of the market. He recognised the uniform as that of the guard of the Palazzo della Signoria, and immediately realised that they were hunting him and his brother. He thought briefly whether to keep his head down and hope that the guards either would not notice them or did not have a description of their quarry, but fear got the better of him.

He tapped Silvio on the shoulder and nodded in the direction of the guards. "We'd better run, brother. We're safer if we separate – you should go and hide in San Marco church. I'll head the opposite way and try to get back to San Miniato. I'll come and find you at San Marco when it's safe."

As they stood up, nerves kicked in and Silvio

knocked over the bench they were sitting on. The guards looked over at the noise and instantly knew these two were their targets. The brothers went in their different directions, and the guards automatically separated into pairs to follow each of them. Silvio sprinted straight across the market, and was small enough to squeeze through the gaps between stalls that lay in long lines in the middle of the market square, thereby quickly losing his chasers. He ran past the Baptistery then away from the cathedral of Santa Maria del Fiore to seek refuge in the church of San Marco, another seat of the Dominican monks.

Marco had a harder job escaping, as he did not have the benefit of making his way through the market stalls. He ran towards the Mercato Nuovo, but this was more open than the old market and offered little cover. He continued at full speed towards Santa Trinità bridge. While crossing the bridge, he took the opportunity to glance back and could see that he had put more ground between himself and the lumbering guards. At the end of the bridge, he turned left down Borgo San Jacopo which was lined with inns whose customers crowded the alley.

This helped him to open the gap between him and the guards still further and he started to feel more confident that he would reach the church. He was looking round to see whether he was still being chased when he stumbled into the four guards who were searching the south side of the river. They grabbed hold of him to tell him to slow down - as Marco was on his own, they did not immediately realise that he was one of the youths they were looking for until the two chasing guards caught up. Marco then knew that he was in trouble, and could only think of the lions he had seen earlier.

The reality was perhaps worse. It took hours of agony before the eighteen year old died on the Strappado. He first had to wait in heavy chains in the Camera delle Arme for Tedesco to complete his dying moments as the sun set, before being hoisted aloft himself. Scalieri refused to believe Marco's preposterous story that the Prior at San Miniato had commanded him and his young brother to write anti-establishment slogans on the walls of the Salone. Marco tried to explain how they only drew the crude pictures because they were incapable of writing the slogans as instructed. Scalieri attached weights to Marco's feet to pull an alternative truth out of him but none came.

Marco finally drew his last breath in pain not long before dawn, while young Silvio slept fitfully in the sanctuary offered by the monks of the church bearing his brother's name, unaware that he was now completely alone in the world.

CHAPTER 8

That evening, three floors above Marco's suffering, a great feast took place for the Ferraresi. After dinner, the guests were invited to stand at the windows that looked out on to the Piazza della Signoria, to watch a display of *fuochi artificiali*, artificial fires, an impressive sequence of explosions and rockets propelled by gunpowder. The whole square was lit up by the fires that were left once the bombs had exploded. A residence on the other side of the river was set on fire when one of the rockets landed on it, causing a great cheer from the watching audience.

Machiavelli broke away in disgust at the lack of sensitivity to his people, and ordered a courtier to send Scalieri to his office to provide an update on the investigations. Scalieri pulled himself away from the Strappado to report his earlier discovery that there had been two intruders and that one of them had been caught and was currently being questioned. He did not mention that it was one of his own guards that had allowed them to intrude. Machiavelli was informed that, under torture, the criminal had so far refused to tell Scalieri why he had painted obscenities on the wall. Scalieri was, while vindictive, a deeply religious man who felt it too shameful to repeat the claim that a Dominican Prior was behind it all.

Not feeling particularly enlightened by Scalieri's account, Machiavelli returned to the festivities in time for their conclusion. The Florentine government gave each member of the delegation from Ferrara a personalised gift, such as their own coat of arms woven in fine silk, or a small marble statue, and wished them well on their journey onwards to Rome. Before they left, Machiavelli was able to impart the news that they had caught the main wrongdoer, who even now was being punished with appropriate severity for the insult caused to the Duke and his men, for which he apologised once again.

After their departure, Soderini and Machiavelli retired to the Gonfaloniere's office to discuss whether their conference and hospitality during the rest of the day had managed to make up for the earlier embarrassment. Naturally their talk turned to the crime itself. Machiavelli relayed the message from Captain Scalieri that the attack appeared to be without reason.

This did not come as a great surprise to Soderini. "My security advisers tell me there has been a wave of misbehaviour in our City this past week. There have been eighteen thefts recorded from great households, including the Pitti's last night, causing Messer Pitti great embarrassment at the Corsini dinner. I have received reports of the murder of three wool merchants and the proprietor of a silk-dying shop in Santa Croce, and of the rape of four fine ladies, whose dignity I will harm no more by repeating their names to you. Plus our buildings seem to have developed an unusual propensity to self-combust."

Machiavelli considered. "While these events individually are not entirely unusual in our City, for them all to occur in the space of a week suggests two things to me. Either there has been a sudden immigration of criminals to our City, or there is something sinister behind these events. I do not believe that so many wrong-doers could suddenly have passed the guards that we have placed at the City gates, so I am forced to look for a more remote cause."

"What do you mean?" asked Soderini.

"That someone must be behind these events, and whoever that is has some motive for causing them to happen. In my view, it is most likely to be the Medici – after numerous attempts at forcing their way back into the City, they may have resorted to more underhand tactics, to destabilise the City and its government and win a popular recall. But there are many other people who would benefit from the City becoming weaker. Venetian silk-merchants for example would love to see the end of the Florentine silk trade. Or it could be a ploy of the Pisans in their constant and ill-considered struggle against us. The French may think that we are becoming too "liberated" for their liking. The attacks seem to be against the rich or the establishment – Savonarola's followers could be behind them. Even the Pope does not trust us and would like more direct control."

"Enough!" interjected Soderini. "You are merely speculating, without any evidence. Pitti told me this morning that he also suspects the Medici clan, but I, who know the family well having served under Lorenzo il Magnifico, am sure that despite their ruthlessness and their desire to return to Florence, petty transgressions such as these are not their style."

"Gonfaloniere, I'm just considering all the possible reasons for this outbreak of pestilence. Unless we understand the cause, we cannot hope to counter the effect. You are right that I have no evidence, and that is what we need. We must be vigilant, and make every attempt to catch and interrogate the perpetrators of these misdemeanors. I will instruct the City Police to double their efforts to apprehend offenders, and to keep them alive so that Scalieri can extract the facts on the *Strappado*. We will soon put a stop to this once the criminals hear that their brethren are squealing and then dying."

Machiavelli talked with an air of quiet confidence that made Soderini feel he must be right about the crimes being linked. Reasoning was, along with art and classical scholarship, one of the main developments of the past century in Florence, and it was still only just being mastered by the most intelligent individuals. Before its reappearance (having last been prevalent in the classical world), unexplained events were seen as pre-ordained, usually by the hand of God. Those who, as Soderini just had, heard people using reasoning in their arguments, could not help being impressed and swayed by it. Unsurprisingly, the doctrines of reasoning were not welcomed by the more religious elements of the Florentine community, who foresaw that the development of such thoughts could pose a threat to the all-powerful position enjoyed by their deity.

"Very well," responded Soderini after pausing to

digest the argument that Machiavelli had put forward, "but you must ensure that it is done *con sottigliezza*, subtly. I do not want the City panicked by the thought that there is some dark force at work. You will mention your reasons to no-one, simply give the orders that security must be tightened and the criminals caught. You are a clever man, Niccolò, I want you to deal with the interrogations personally and find the root of this evil to justify your assertions."

Machiavelli knew that Soderini was his match for intelligence, even if he had not studied some of the newer philosophies. Soderini had just laid down a challenge for Machiavelli to prove his argument – the stakes for Machiavelli were now high. If he should fail to produce results, he knew that after a while he would start to be blamed for the rise in offences. Florentine politics made for a cruel game – if you stuck your head above the parapet, it was there to be shot at. While Soderini would not tell others directly that Machiavelli had a misconceived theory, he would certainly start a series of leaks of information, and soon rumours would find their way on to the stickers posted on walls throughout the City, from which the citizens gathered the latest (if not always accurate) news.

By placing the responsibility for stopping the rot with Machiavelli, Soderini knew that not only did he have his best man on the job, but also if the ringleaders were not found, he could make any blame rest with Machiavelli. If Machiavelli managed to prove his theory, and stop the crime wave, Soderini could take the praise for having appointed the man who solved the problem, and claim ultimate responsibility. The normally dour Soderini permitted himself a small smile, unseen by the other man.

The following morning, Machiavelli summoned Scalieri and Captain Giannini, the chief of the City police, to his office in the Palazzo della Signoria. He did not entirely agree with Soderini's view that the reasons behind his orders should be kept secret, but he had little choice but to follow the command for the time being. He would have liked to tell these two, so that they would have a better idea of how to set their men to the task.

He didn't like either of the men very much, and even though they had proved themselves to be two of the most trust-worthy individuals in Florence, he knew that if he told either captain, they could easily let something slip to a senior officer, and from there a story would spread like wild-fire. Better just to give the orders.

"Giannini, please could you explain to me what the City police are doing at the moment." Better still to get the chief of police feeling guilty first about the lack of arrests.

"Messer Machiavelli, I have all my men deployed around the City looking out for the people who have been carrying out the recent felonies, and they are working extra shifts," responded Giannini sheepishly. He knew that Machiavelli's line of questioning was likely to lead somewhere he did not want to go.

"Do they know what the criminals look like then?" asked Machiavelli.

"No, but it is easy to spot them, as they will show the give-away signs of being *stranieri*, people from outside the City, and they will be looking shifty. We have already arrested a dozen suspects."

"Do you have confessions from any of them?"

"We are working on that Messer Machiavelli. We have only two Strappado frames at *Le Stinche*, and it is taking some time to extract information from these men, as they are experienced criminals with tight tongues."

"And how many have died on your Strappado without giving a confession?" Machiavelli continued to probe.

"Four Messer," Giannini was feeling more uncomfortable with every answer, knowing twelve arrests, four deaths and no information did not look encouraging.

"And you," Machiavelli turned to Scalieri, "how did you let that young man die yesterday without obtaining anything useful from him?"

Scalieri struggled with the shame that he was being exposed to by Machiavelli, compared with the shame of telling him that he believed the Dominicans were involved. Scalieri did not like Giannini, and would go out of his way to get one up on him (the feeling was mutual), but he drew the line at implicating the Church. "He was small and weak, and it took very little time for his life to be exhausted under pressure."

Machiavelli had the men where he wanted them – embarrassed and well aware of the need to produce results. "Giannini, I want you to order your men to arrest all known criminals on sight, whether they are *stranieri* or *Fiorentini*. Throw them all in prison. The crime will stop, and the rumours will start. Put some of your own men in the prisons, disguised as low-life. They will pick up on the rumours and you will be able to identify the criminals."

Giannini and Scalieri could only marvel at the plan, recognising that they would never have thought of such calculating methods. Giannini was about to object that the prisons could not hold all those people, but he realised that the more crowded the conditions were, the quicker results would be in coming. He was not bothered by the thought that his own men would undoubtedly pick up fatal afflictions while incarcerated alongside the criminals.

"And what shall I do?" asked Scalieri.

"Nothing," replied Machiavelli. Another part of his plan was to give Giannini the opportunity to outshine Scalieri. The enmity between the two captains was well-known, and was something that Machiavelli could exploit. It stemmed from the battle in which Scalieri had sustained his injury. Scalieri had been a captain in the mercenary army raised by the City, and Giannini a foot-soldier in his unit. Scalieri had stood and fought the invaders, while many of his soldiers, Giannini included, had turned and fled when they saw the number of well equipped French and Milanese troops that confronted them.

Scalieri's wound stagnated his career – being in charge of a few guards at the Palazzo della Signoria was nothing compared with the leadership of the City's police. Florence was unusual in having a standing police force, but it was another institution that had been instigated by the Medici. Initially they had used it as a tool to enforce their own will on the City. But as the force's numbers had grown, it had taken on a more independent position to avoid being criticised for bias by the City's other powerful families. Scalieri had watched Giannini's rise through the ranks of the police with growing disgust.

Machiavelli also knew that if he expressly gave all the responsibility to Giannini, Scalieri would go out of his way to get his own results in order to outshine the other man. This way he would obtain the best performance from both men.

CHAPTER 9

Having laboured at a frenetic pace to complete their work at the new Corsini palace, Anziani and Donato were spending a few days relaxing at Anziani's home before starting to look for new employment. Donato was surprised when a messenger called at the door for him. He was even more surprised to hear from the messenger an invitation to attend Federico Benvenuti's palace the next day. Once the messenger had departed, Donato asked Anziani what he knew of Benvenuti. "Apart from that he's the richest man in town? Not a lot. He must keep himself to himself, as he never seems to be the subject of gossip. I've heard people saying that he's aloof to the point of being sinister, but I wouldn't know."

Donato wondered what motive might lie behind the invitation. He had seen Benvenuti looking over at him while in conversation with Corsini that evening, and laughing. Donato suspected that his arrival at Benvenuti's palace would be followed by some kind of humiliation, but he did not dare to speculate as to its form. Even so, having received an invitation from such an important figure, attendance was obligatory.

It was raining when Donato left Anziani's house for his appointment with Benvenuti. Donato liked the rain. The monotonous pitter-patter it made when it fell from the roofs on to the ground beneath was somehow comforting to him. The grey stones that paved the streets were turned a shiny black, like polished granite, and the usual hubbub of the City was eerily hushed by the low cloud and water in the air and on the ground.

The palace overlooked Piazza Santa Maria Novella, near where Donato had spent his first night in the City. On arrival, Donato was shown into an ante-room by one of Benvenuti's footmen, without a word being said. As the morning passed without any further human appearance, Donato's suspicions about the motives behind the invitation grew, although at least he could dry out a little from the soaking received on his way across the City.

Eventually, the footman who had opened the door to him invited Donato into Benvenuti's audience room. The owner was sitting behind a large, ornately carved and beautifully inlaid wooden desk. The first thing Donato noticed about the man now that he was able to see him up close was his pair of icy blue eyes piercing straight through him. Donato surmised from the colour that Benvenuti must be from the mountainous north of Italy, as Tuscans only had olive or chestnut eyes, matching two of their main crops.

When Benvenuti spoke, however, it was with a perfect Florentine accent. "Thank you for coming. I am sorry I did not have the opportunity to speak to you at Corsini's the other night. He was very enthusiastic about your abilities, and I invited you here today because I have some work I would like you to do."

"But you haven't even seen my work, how do you know I would be suitable?" Donato protested, thrown off-balance by Benvenuti's apparently warm approach.

"If I don't like what you do for me, I will have it re-done by another artist, and you will never work in Florence again." *There's the catch*, thought Donato. *This man is so powerful that if I produce anything less than perfect, my career here will be finished before it's even started. On the other hand, if the work is good, who knows where it may take me?*

"What do you want me to do?" Donato asked abruptly, having still not recovered his composure.

"You will paint the chapel that has just been built at the back of this palace." There seemed no choice in the matter. Benvenuti continued "I will pay you a hundred gold florins. I need the painting finished within two months."

"May I see the building please?" asked Donato, finally thinking a little more rationally, despite having just been offered more money than he had ever seen.

"Yes, of course. You cannot accept such a challenge without seeing what you have to work with," replied Benvenuti. He pulled a chord behind his desk, and Donato heard a bell ring loudly in the next room. Benvenuti's head servant suddenly appeared at the door of the office, and Benvenuti shouted a command to him to take Donato to see the chapel and then return him to the office.

As Donato scurried along the long corridors of the

palace trying to keep up with the surprisingly sprightly old servant, he reflected on what he had just heard. Benvenuti appeared generous and understanding, yet Donato sensed a darker ruthless side to him, capable of inflicting great harm if crossed. He would be a difficult master, but for a hundred florins Donato decided he could cope with anyone, even before seeing the chapel.

Donato was so deep in thought that he did not notice anything of the insides of the palace, and he barely saw Benvenuti's beautiful daughter Chiara pass him. The servant led him out into the enclosed garden and over to the chapel at its far side. It was, thankfully, a small building, not more than twenty-five *braccie*, lengths of an arm, square, with a high ceiling. Inside, it was almost exactly a cube, with a recess opposite the door for the altar, and another on one side for the confessional.

Donato was now becoming so excited at the thought of having his first real commission that he absorbed very little detail of the building. He wanted to get back to Benvenuti and discuss themes for the chapel. The servant said nothing from leaving the office until their return.

Back in the office Benvenuti asked whether Donato had studied the chapel in the old Palazzo dei Medici, painted by Benozzo Gozzoli forty years previously, on which Benvenuti wanted the painting in his own chapel modelled. Donato admitted that he had not. Since the Medici had left the City, their palace had first been stripped of all its great treasures by Savonarola's followers, and then taken over by the state. Using his commercial and political influence, Benvenuti was able to secure entry to the chapel for Donato, and insisted that before he start on any designs he spend a week there drinking in its qualities.

The Medici family had, in the fifty years they had occupied the palace, filled it with ancient Roman and Greek sculptures as well as contemporary pieces of art and craftsmanship. Although the palace was sacked as one of the first acts of the new republic in 1494, the frescoed chapel, showing the Procession of the Magi to Bethlehem, survived due to its religious nature, even though many of the figures depicted were actually portraits of the Medici and members of their court.

Benvenuti wanted Donato to produce a fresco cycle in a similar way, based on the story of Moses leading the Jews out of Egypt. Old testament cycles were less usual, but this story gave Benvenuti the chance to be portrayed as Moses himself, a great leader of the people from a time of adversity to one of prosperity, which was where his own ambitions lay.

Benvenuti's plan was to start putting the impression into citizens' minds that he was the person who could lead them back to the City's heyday under Lorenzo il Magnifico. He would climb the ladder of power through a combination of political manoeuvring and tactical distribution of favours and money. But he would strive assiduously to ensure that he was not associated with any physical crime (as opposed to bribery and corruption), conscious that most of the Florentine people would not tolerate overt violence. He wanted to reach a position where he could launch a dynasty to rival the Medici. It would be a legacy to pass on to his four year old son, who had arrived as a great surprise many years after the birth of

Chiara.

"You will, of course, stay here until the job is done, so that you can work at all times" continued Benvenuti. Although Donato knew that this was standard practice, he could not believe that the offer was getting better and better. "Will you accept?"

"I would be honoured to do so, yes sir. I only hope I can do justice to your vision," Donato replied quietly, experiencing a sudden and unusual crisis in confidence now that he knew that there would be enormous pressure on him to produce a chapel that would rival that in the palace of the Medici. Apart from his recent involvement with the Corsini place, he had never undertaken a project on such a scale, let alone on his own. Would he be able to delivery to Benvenuti's exacting standards, or would he fall flat on his face and find his Florentine venture at a premature end?

Donato raced back to Anziani's house to gather his few belongings together. He waited for Anziani to return from work, to give him the news and to thank him for his generosity and support.

Anziani was delighted for his young friend, but warned jokingly "Promise to stay in touch, and don't become big-headed once you start moving in elevated circles." Anziani knew that this could be the making of Donato, and was more than he had achieved in his entire lifetime of painting in Florence, but his good wishes were not tinged with any jealousy. In the short time that Donato had been living with him, Anziani had started to feel like an uncle towards the boy.

Donato ran back to the Benvenuti palace before nightfall, and was shown to his small but clean room in the servants' quarters – although the stock of artists was rising, patrons still treated their resident artists as part of their working staff.

The following morning, Donato rose early and went straight to the former palace of the Medici on Via Larga, passing by the Medici's family church of San Lorenzo with its market stalls selling textiles and leathers on the square outside. The palace was now occupied by government offices, and Benvenuti had sent notice to the palace guards the previous afternoon that they were to admit Donato to the chapel for a week. He was ushered straight up the stairs to the small painted room. As he entered he was dazzled by the vibrant colours adorning the four walls. He had brought plenty of paper and charcoal, and he immediately sat himself on the marble floor in the middle of the room, eschewing the uncomfortable looking wooden seats around the walls, and started sketching.

Although the chapel was small, similar in size to the one he had been asked to paint (was that any coincidence, he wondered), it took him five solid days to record all the painting, so rich was its detail. By the end of the week, Donato had faithfully copied the three main frescoes, showing the processions of Melchior, Balthasar and, most importantly Gaspar, as it was in this fresco that Gozzoli had paid his homage to the Medici, as well as including his own face looking out from the crowd.

He returned to his room in the Benvenuti palace each evening elated yet exhausted. The hours of sitting in the centre of the room, with his neck craned upwards to view the paintwork, were so absorbing that he did not notice his limbs stiffen, or mealtimes pass. He was only disturbed by the chaplain replacing the candles half-way through each day – a hundred were needed to give him sufficient light, as there were no windows in the Medici's chapel.

He ate each night with the palace servants, typical Florentine fare of stewed beans and meat, mopped up with hard bread and washed down with weak red wine. He pinned his sketches of the chapel around his room at the palace, so that he lived and breathed the work.

When Donato returned from his final day at the Medici palace, Benvenuti called him into the office once again. "I am pleased with the dedication you have shown so far, and with the astuteness with which you have observed Gozzoli's work. I am confident that your decoration of my chapel will be successful, but my wife has suggested that you will need a greater understanding of me and my family before you can embark on the task of painting us in the correct light. Unlike most wives, she has nasty a habit of always being right.

"I am therefore arranging for your possessions to be moved into the residential rooms, and you will eat with us each evening. I will pay you a weekly advance of five florins, and you must dress yourself appropriately. My chamber servant will take you to my tailor in the morning."

Donato tried to ignore the fact that Benvenuti had evidently been into his room to study the drawings. "Thank you Messer. I am but a simple boy, and I do not feel able to grace your table with conversation of high things, or to live as part of your court. I must therefore respectfully decline your kind invitation. I will see you enough on your business about the palace."

"Nonsense," Benvenuti retorted quietly but firmly. "It is done." Donato realised that, once again, he had no choice but to accept his new position. Benvenuti handed over the first instalment of money to seal the deal.

The next day, Donato obediently went to the tailor for three sets of dinner-wear. While the servant waited at the tailor's for the first set of clothes to be completed so that Donato could wear them that night, Donato proceeded to Nello's for a fresh hair-cut and shave. It was a working day, so he did not expect to see Messer Corsini coming out of the barber's shop as he arrived.

"What are you doing here?" asked Corsini.

Donato looked sheepish, knowing that Corsini would feel that he owed him some allegiance. "I have just been offered my first commission, and thought I should give myself a tidy up."

Corsini looked like he was about to explode. "After all I have done for you, you have taken work from somebody else without even having the decency to speak to me about it?" Corsini's fury brought back to Donato the memory of that first morning when the old man found him sleeping in his palace.

"Yes sir, I am sorry, I did not think."

"I could have handed you over to the authorities when you broke into my building, but instead I was persuaded by your youthful enthusiasm to give you a chance and let you work for me, giving you the start that you needed in this City and introducing you to Anziani. And this is how you repay me?

"I am not a vengeful man, but I can only say that I am bitterly disappointed. I thought you would have even a little more loyalty."

Corsini left in high dudgeon, without even enquiring who Donato was going to work for – he would have been even more angry had he known that it was Benvenuti. Donato went in through Nello's door, but the barber threw him straight back out again. "I'm sorry young man, but Messer Corsini is one of my most important customers. I have just heard the dishonourable way in which you have treated him. I can give you no welcome in my humble shop."

Donato stumbled out, barely able to see through the tears of shame that welled in his eyes.

That evening, Donato sat in embarrassed silence at the dinner table with Benvenuti, his wife Maria, and Chiara. Benvenuti's young son spent most of his time with his nursemaid, and did not eat with the family. The first thing Donato noticed on entering the room was Chiara's outstanding beauty. She wore a long yellow dress which plunged at the breast showing a well-developed cleavage. The bust of her dress was cut so tightly that it caused her breasts to rise and fall with her every breath. Her hair, held up in a bunch by a gold band but with a few enticing curls escaping, was chestnut brown, matching her wide and clear eyes, inherited from her mother. When she smiled on being introduced by her father, she showed a set of perfect straight white teeth sitting between full and soft lips. Donato guessed she must have been a year or two younger than himself. He did not know where to look, conscious that he should not betray any feelings of desire for the girl.

Benvenuti tried to speak to Donato about his ideas for the painting of the chapel, which Donato would start on

Monday. The older man swiftly realised, however, that Donato was incapable of coherent speech and thought the boy was simply overawed by the occasion of his first dinner with the family, so he dropped the subject.

CHAPTER 10

On the Saturday before Donato began his engagement for Benvenuti, Leonardo Vinci was in his new workshop, directly across the square in the monastery behind the church of Santa Maria Novella. He was wrapping up in linen, ready for delivery, a portrait of the wife of a Florentine silk trader, having completed it just the previous evening.

He had been painting it, off and on, for nearly three years, and although his client had only commissioned a small portrait, Leonardo had encountered great difficulty in reaching a result that he was happy with. Two features of the picture bothered Leonardo in particular. He had had to repaint the background several times as he developed a new technique that he called '*sfumato*' or 'smoky'. And he just could not get the woman's mouth right.

But he had finally decided that he had spent too much time on an unimportant client so he would deliver the picture as it was. He now had to devote his time to a far bigger and more important project.

The workshop had been provided to him by the Signoria as part of his commission for a large fresco to adorn one of the walls in the Salone dei Cinquecento, which would depict, typically, a great Florentine battle victory. This was the most important public commission since the Signoria had asked Michelangelo Buonarroti to produce the enormous statue of David three years previously. As the David now neared completion, Leonardo was being given the opportunity to eclipse it, a fact which angered Michelangelo greatly.

Today, however, Leonardo was more concerned with delivering the portrait to his private patron. It was a fine spring morning, and Leonardo decided to walk down to the river with one of his assistants, Piero da Gavine, to enjoy the sunshine which was cut out by the tall buildings hanging menacingly over the narrow streets away from the Arno. He was in a bright mood, and accordingly wore a billowy pink shirt with sky blue hose.

Leonardo's customer, along with many other silk traders, lived in the Santa Croce district, a pleasant walk along the Lungarno past the City's four bridges. The artist carried the wrapped poplar wood panel which bore the painting himself rather than risking it in the hands of his assistant.

As the pair passed the entrance to the second of those bridges, Ponte a Santa Trinità, da Gavine was hailed by Anziani, who had worked with him on a number of occasions and knew him well. Anziani was standing with a group of friends, which included Donato, outside the Palazzo Spini. Da Gavine and his master walked over to join the group – the purpose of a fine Saturday morning in Florence was to do nothing other than stand around talking of politics, literature, art and women.

Today's topic was the second of those. The group immediately recognised the man with da Gavine as Leonardo – his face was well-known, but none of them had actually met him. Da Gavine and Anziani made introductions, with Anziani's companions, including the young Donato, blushing with embarrassment to be meeting the famous Leonardo in person.

The group were discussing a confusing passage from Dante's Inferno, and Anziani asked da Gavine's view. Just then, Michelangelo approached over the bridge, on his own, carrying a heavy sack over his shoulder.

Michelangelo's talent had first been spotted at the age of thirteen, when he was apprenticed to Domenico Ghirlandaio. He swiftly came to the attention of Lorenzo Il Magnifico, who gave him a place to study at the Medici's own academy. The primary purpose of this was to improve his artistic skills, but the academy also provided a more rounded education, including Latin, Ancient Greek, philosophy and literature, so that an artist should better understand the themes he would be working on for the rest of his life.

Leonardo knew that Michelangelo was not the sort of person who would have enjoyed academic study. Always on the lookout for mischief, he now spotted an opportunity to wind up his competitor. He shouted over to the younger artist "Here comes a scholar, he'll explain it for you."

Michelangelo had broken his last chisel earlier that morning while working on his statue of David, and was now on his way back from his iron-monger on the other side of the river having picked up some more iron to make new chisels. He made all his own tools, but was still annoyed at having been distracted from his work at a crucial stage.

Renowned for his abrasiveness at the best of times, Michelangelo did not have time to engage in frivolous conversation. Neither did he appreciate Leonardo putting him on the spot like that. While the others took Leonardo's invitation to join the debate as well-meaning, Michelangelo knew that it was barbed. Although the two artists held a begrudging respect for each other's talents, there was certainly no friendship. Indeed, there was positive animosity between them since Leonardo had won the commission for the Signoria fresco.

Michelangelo shot sharply back at Leonardo, without even enquiring as to what was under discussion, "Explain it yourself, you who designed a horse to be cast in bronze, could not cast it, and so shamefully abandoned it."

If Michelangelo was known for his abrasiveness, Leonardo was known for taking on many projects and completing few, often distracted by his scientific, rather than artistic, pursuits. Michelangelo's piqued response had been calculated to hit a raw nerve, referring to one of Leonardo's most notorious failures, a project for a giant bronze statue of the Duke of Milan on horseback.

"Go and retch!" retorted Leonardo. He was so furious at being spoken to like that by the upstart Michelangelo, and at being embarrassed in front of his young acquaintances, that he immediately stormed back to his workshop with the portrait still under his arm. There the painting would remain, as Leonardo never delivered it to his client, Francesco del Giocondo, and his wife, Monna Lisa.

CHAPTER 11

When Donato began work in the chapel on Monday, he found it difficult to get the vision of Chiara out of his mind. He spent much of the day walking between the palace and the chapel taking over his sketches and all the tools and materials that Benvenuti had procured for him, hoping for any passing glimpse of Chiara, but he did not see her.

Donato set up a large table on trestles in the centre of the chapel, on which he could draw his initial ideas for the painting. He would have to get these preparatory drawings approved by his master before making more detailed cartoons to the scale of the final fresco. He would then apply the layer of *intonaco* plaster to a wall. The *intonaco* had to be painted while still wet in order for it to hold the paint properly. It was impossible to draw any outline for the painting on to wet plaster so the artist would pin the cartoons for that wall over the plaster, apply the basic pattern of the drawings through the paper using ivory needles to make indentations in the *intonaco*, remove the cartoons and paint on to the plaster underneath before it dried.

This was a laborious process, as only a small part of each wall could be painted at any time before the plaster dried out. But the benefit of using the cartoons in this way was that he could ensure that scale and perspective were kept perfect, which was nigh on impossible if painting freehand on to a large wall. Painting on to wet plaster kept the colours much more vibrant, as the paints became part of the fabric of the wall.

When the light that came through the chapel's door and narrow windows faded so that he could no longer see to draw, Donato retreated to Benvenuti's well-lit library to read about the story of Moses from the Bible and other ancient sources before changing for dinner with the family. As the nights passed, he became more at ease at the dinner table, able to talk about his family in Lucca, and to discuss themes for the chapel. He still consciously averted his eyes from Chiara, but just occasionally she caught him looking at her and he looked away shyly. She started to engage him in conversation about Florentine life, and soon his self-consciousness started to wane.

One dinner in the second week of Donato's sojourn at the palace, Chiara asked her father whether she could watch Donato at work in the Chapel. "You'll have to ask the man himself – he may prefer to work alone," was the response.

"Donato, will you allow me to observe as you create your first masterpiece?"

Donato thought she was teasing him, and so put

his head down without responding.

Chiara continued, oblivious to his reaction. "I promise not to be intrusive. Please feel free to say no if you think my presence will inhibit your work, but I would so much like to see an artist at work, and the genesis of the decoration of my father's chapel."

Donato realised that Chiara was being earnest in her request. But he knew that to have Chiara in the chapel with him would make it enormously difficult for him to concentrate on the task in hand. Even if he could not see her, he would be conscious of her proximity and the smell of her sweet perfume would fill his nose. Once again, however, he felt obliged to accede to the request, as to deny it would look churlish. And although he knew her being there would conflict with his ability to do his work, he was excited about the possibility of being left alone with Benvenuti's daughter.

"I would be honoured," was all he could say.

Donato had not contemplated that, when she arrived at the chapel mid-morning the next day, Chiara would be accompanied by the head servant who had shown him there that first day. Of course the master would not allow her to attend the chapel with a young artist without a chaperone – how foolish to imagine otherwise. Even so, Chiara's presence in the room, without her parents, excited Donato. He tried to concentrate on the task in hand, but found himself shaking as he attempted to draw a cartoon of Moses leading the Israelites across the Red Sea.

Chiara could see that the artist was uncomfortable, and left without a word, the servant following silently in tow. Her departure confused Donato – was she angry at him for ignoring her, or had she seen his discomfort and so left out of kindness? He had not dared speak to her that morning, for fear that the servant would be under instructions to report everything back to Benvenuti. He wanted, above all, to impress Benvenuti with his diligence and dedication, and any news of him talking to his guest would indicate distraction. In any event, he had no idea how he might open a conversation with her.

Chiara did not come to the chapel the next day, and Donato thought that he must have offended her with his cold shoulder. He cursed himself for not having the imagination or courage to be able to speak freely to her. He was now even more distracted without her than he had been in her presence, as her whole being – her beautiful face, her delicate voice, her curvaceous body, her rolling hair, her gentle countenance and her warm aroma - filled and tormented his mind. He felt her absence as if the whole world had collapsed on him.

Donato did not mention what was preying on his mind over dinner that night, and he made sure not to look at Chiara throughout the meal. When he retired to bed, he turned it over and over in his mind and could not sleep. He realised that his few brief encounters with Chiara had resulted in an obsession. He resolved to work through it – if she did not come to the chapel again, he would always see her at dinner, and would have to slake his thirst for her company there. Her absence would also give him the opportunity to include Chiara's image in his fresco, perhaps as an angel.

The next day, Donato still dared to hope that Chiara would come to the chapel, but his wish went unfulfilled, as it did for the rest of the week.

It was not until the following Monday, while Donato was drawing an Egyptian chariot getting bogged down in marshland, that Chiara arrived once more, again with her escort. Donato was by now exhausted from the lack of sleep caused by his inability to turn his thoughts away from the girl. His heart leapt into his mouth when he saw her, and this time he conquered his nerves to say a curt "Good morning."

Chiara returned his simple greeting with a courteous smile, and sat on the chair that her servant had brought. Thereafter, as on her previous visit, no word was spoken, but Chiara stayed for longer, only leaving when another servant brought Donato his usual lunch of bread and hard cheese. Over the course of the morning Donato gradually started to feel more at ease in her company, and his lines became straighter as he shook less.

Donato noted that he had not ever heard the head servant speak, despite having seen him on several occasions, and that whenever anyone spoke to the man they shouted and gesticulated even more than usual for Florentines. He realised that the servant must be deaf.

That night at dinner, Benvenuti asked Chiara how Donato's work was coming along.

"Donato works hard, but there seems to be no progress in painting the walls." Donato reddened with embarrassment, but Benvenuti laughed.

"It will be many weeks before our master artist is ready to start addressing the walls," he said. "First, he must complete the preparatory drawings and have them all approved by me." Donato said nothing.

When Chiara arrived the next day, Donato was emboldened by her father's support and her own ignorance of the process of creating a fresco cycle. He felt able to engage her in a little more conversation, and explain what he was doing. "Before I start painting the walls, I must have a complete picture of what will be on them, so that I know all the walls fit with each other. When your father has settled on my designs, then I will start painting the walls themselves."

"What are you designing now?" asked Chiara.

"I'm working on the same image that I was when you first came here, Moses leading the Israelites through the Red Sea, which I propose to paint on the south wall of the chapel given Egypt's position to the south of Israel." Donato did not tell her that the reason he had been unable to move beyond that image was Chiara herself. He just couldn't get the drawings right, and was on his umpteenth version of the same event.

"Will you permit me to look?" ventured Chiara.

"You are part of my master's family, so I must permit you to look if you ask to do so," was Donato's guarded response. He did not want Chiara to see the cartoon in its current state, but as was so frequently the case in the Benvenuti household, he also felt that he effectively had no choice in the matter.

Chiara walked playfully round to Donato's side of his work-bench, and requested a more detailed explanation of the drawing.

Donato spoke *sottovoce* so that Chiara's deaf companion would be certain of not hearing. "This," he said, pointing to a figure floating in the top right corner of the picture, "is going to be the angel of the Lord who guided Moses through the sea. As I permitted you to look, perhaps you would do me the honour of allowing me to model the angel's face on your own. I was going to paint your face there anyway, but as you have come to me, I should take this opportunity to seek your consent. You see, you have the face of an angel, and it cried out to me to be painted here."

Donato stopped himself as he saw Chiara blushing for the first time and realised he had spoken what he had meant to keep to himself. "I'm sorry, I should not have said that. Please don't repeat it to your father."

"No, you should not have said that, but I am flattered, so yes, I agree to you painting me. Will you need me to model for you?" Donato was astounded by the openness of Chiara's whispered response. The pair had their heads down over the work-bench, so there was no danger of the servant reading their words from their lips. Donato felt a new frisson of excitement leap through his body, and fought once again to keep calm.

He could not now admit that her offer to model for him was unnecessary because he had memorised, with his artist's eye, every feature of her face. Chiara's father would be sitting for him on many occasions, to capture Moses in different moods, so why not Chiara? What would Benvenuti do if he found out that his daughter was posing for Donato? Would it be better to seek his permission, or to try to paint Chiara covertly? Word would be bound to get back to his master, and even if it did not, Benvenuti would recognise his daughter in the finished fresco – what would he say then? Benvenuti was highly protective of his daughter, and would not want Donato studying her to the level of detail necessary to produce a fine likeness.

The idea then came to Donato that it would be better not to have her sitting formally at all. If he could just observe her as she watched him at his work, he might pick up a more natural version of the girl than were she to pose. He would draw a different face for the angel in the drawings for presentation to Benvenuti and in the subsequent preparatory cartoons, so that Chiara's face would only be recognisable in the final painting.

After what seemed to Donato like an eternity of consideration, he eventually spoke. "No, that will not be necessary. I can draw the inspiration that I need simply from your presence here when it suits you." He was pleased with this – it was complimentary yet reserved and proper.

"Very well, I shall see you tomorrow," Chiara closed the conversation and left abruptly. Donato sensed a little irritation in her rapid departure, which reminded him of the reactions of his younger sister back in Lucca when she was told to do something against her will. He dismissed it as a typical reaction of a girl of that age.

Later in the day, though, Chiara returned to the chapel, this time alone. As Donato had become more at ease with her, so she had started to develop feelings for him. She found his long angular face, framed by a mop of brown hair that had swiftly reverted to its usual unkempt state since his only successful visit to Nello the barber, strangely appealing. But she had never spent any significant time in the company of a boy of her age, and she could not understand the butterflies that she now felt in her stomach every time she saw him in the chapel or over dinner.

She wanted to find out whether Donato had the same problem, so she crept through the corridors of the palace, unseen by the servants or her mother, across the garden and into the chapel. Donato sensed her arrival, but carried on drawing, as he had by now become accustomed to her presence. She approached, and put a hand gently on his shoulder.

He turned around and their eyes met briefly before they both looked away in embarrassment. Chiara took a step back, and felt too afraid to ask Donato about the butterflies. After a brief pause she said "I came to see if you needed a fresh jug of spring-water to drink."

Donato knew that she would normally leave such tasks to the servants, and that she must have come to the chapel for some other reason. He did not want to embarrass her further by challenging her reason for being there, and instead he reached down and took one of her hands. She withdrew it and went to sit in the chair that had been put in one corner of the chapel for her to observe Donato's progress. Without any further words, Donato returned to his drawing, with his back to Chiara, the offer of fresh water forgotten.

Chiara remained in her seat for much of the afternoon, until eventually she plucked up the courage to approach Donato once again. This time she walked round to the other side of his table. She felt a sudden urge to lean down and kiss Donato's head as he still pored over his work, but retained her upright poise.

Donato thought for a moment, then moved to her side of the table and embraced Chiara. Their lips met in a brief but passionate kiss, before Chiara pulled herself away and ran out of the chapel.

CHAPTER 12

As Donato and Chiara embraced in the chapel, Corsini was returning home from an inspection of the final works at his new palace. He walked with an uncharacteristic swagger, as he was rather pleased with himself that afternoon. Not only was his new residence looking extremely impressive, but earlier in the day he had been appointed chairman of Arte della Lana, the Wool-merchants Guild. Florence was run at a commercial level by its twenty-one guilds, of which Arte della Lana, and its great rival Calimala (the Guild of the cloth treaters and traders) were the most important and prestigious.

Corsini had fought hard to be elected. After more than forty years in the wool trade, during which time he had climbed to being the biggest trader in the City, he had still had to spend a small fortune on entertaining the dignatories of Florence over the past twelve months to ensure that he was the best connected of the leadership candidates. He reflected with pride at the effectiveness of his campaign, the culmination of which had been the recent high-powered dinner party.

It certainly helped that in addition to his wool business, he ran a very small and very private bank. Many of the noblemen of Florence were loath to place their money with the big banks, because often such banks were subject to calls from the Pope or, more lately, the Kings of France and England, for large amounts of funds.

The banks were easy targets when a ruler needed money for his next war or to help himself out of some political disaster. They usually succumbed to the enormous pressure put on them to make such loans even when they knew that there was little prospect of repayment and that non-payment may ruin them. Normal customers' deposits with these banks were therefore frequently lost, although large depositors tended to spread their money around different banks in order to reduce their risk.

Corsini's bank only served a dozen customers, so it was beneath the gaze of such tyrants. Consequently, it was a favoured place for some of the richest and most astute men of the City, even those who had their own banks, to keep a portion of their money and treasures. Of course, guarding such people's assets meant that Corsini had to preserve absolute privacy over his accounts, as was the case with all the other banks, but he knew each of his customers, and their finances, personally. Unlike some other bankers, Corsini consciously never used this knowledge to exert any influence over his customers, and they often showed their appreciation for this by supporting him in his activities.

The chairmanship of Arte della Lana would bring him immense political as well as commercial power – the

City relied on the guilds to promulgate its political and economic strategies. The guilds were in a position to make this possible because all workers in the trades covered by a guild had to be members of that guild. If they were not, it was almost impossible to find employment. Once they were members, they had to abide by the strict rules of their guild, and toe any line imparted by the guild's leadership.

Corsini knew that his appointment meant far more than being recognised as one of the most important businessmen in the City. In the past, leadership of Arte della Lana or Calimala had led, for around half of all appointments, to a major role in the government of the City, and often ultimately to election as Gonfaloniere. Even though Corsini was well into his sixties, he had become hungry for new challenges, and felt that a move into politics would provide the change he was looking for, as well as an opportunity to build himself a grander legacy. With a bit of cunning and luck, he could manoeuvre himself into a position where he could challenge for political leadership of the City.

Soderini had been elected as Gonfaloniere for life only two years back, but three things could cut his tenure short. Soderini could meet an untimely death, someone could mount a constitutional challenge to the life-time election, or he could be forced out under threat of arms. Any of those was a distinct possibility in Florence of 1504. Soderini's fall, however occasioned, would precipitate an election for a new leader, and Corsini would be well-placed to stand in any such election within a year or two of taking up his post in Arte della Lana. Not that he had any intention of forcing his friend Soderini out, but if the opportunity arose to succeed him, Corsini would not turn it down.

The man therefore had good reason to be pleased with himself. The world, or Florence at least (to Florentines these were almost the same), was about to be deposited at his feet, there for the taking.

It had been a tough but enjoyable day. The election at the Guild had started the previous midday. Since then, without a break until the decision was made, the twenty men who comprised the Guild's Committee were cocooned in their council chamber.

The time taken was due to the need to follow rules that dated from the twelfth century, requiring the voters to place black beans, for a vote against, or white beans, for a vote in favour, in an embroidered red woollen bag that was passed around the Committee table. The bag went round once for each of the compulsory six candidates, and at the end of each circuit that candidate's beans were counted and noted in secret by the Guild's secretary. Voters could vote in favour of as many candidates as they wished, and at the end of each round, the candidate with the highest number of black beans was announced by the secretary and discarded from the process. Before every round, each candidate would make a speech extolling his virtues, and often raking up muck on his rivals, so each leg of the process could consume hours. These rules were, in Corsini's view, archaic, and were symptomatic of the Guild's decline.

That view was not shared by all of the Guild's committee, and Corsini knew that it would be a considerable challenge over the next few years for him to reform the Guild. It had fallen a little behind Calimala in terms of importance (otherwise known as wealth) over the last century, as witnessed by the quality and quantity of public works of art that the two guilds had respectively commissioned.

Corsini privately maintained that the start of Arte della Lana's decline could be traced precisely to the commissioning of the doors on the eastern entrance to Florence's baptistery at the beginning of the *cuatrocento*, the 1400s, in a competition run by the Calimala and won by Lorenzo Ghiberti. Salt had been rubbed in Arte della Lana's wounds only recently as Michelangelo, on winning the City's commission for the David, proclaimed that he only hoped he could create a piece of similar stature to those doors, which he likened to the Gates to Paradise. Such pronouncements stuck in the public consciousness.

Corsini's election manifesto had been based on reviving his Guild's fortunes, but he had not gone into detail prior to the election as to how he would achieve this, knowing that the electors were mostly traditionalists who would not entertain wholesale change. He won the final election round mid-morning, after which the Committee broke for a celebratory lunch. It was only in his acceptance speech delivered at the end of lunch that Corsini revealed his plans, hatched over many months of thought. He would cut the Committee from twenty members to just five, so that the Guild was less likely to be paralysed by the indecision that had afflicted it over the past hundred years.

All power in the Guild would therefore be concentrated in just five men – fifteen members of the Committee would be disenfranchised. The news caused uproar in the Guild's Hall. The twenty current members of the committee were the twenty biggest wool-merchants in Florence, and not one of them could entertain the thought of losing his place on the committee while five of their number became all the more powerful. After explaining the reasons behind the sudden change – his desire to return the Guild to its glory days - Corsini decided that it would be best to allow them to continue their protests without him, in the hope that the objections would die down eventually.

He had taken leave of the Committee, and gone to his new palace. It was empty of workmen, and he had gratefully paced the central courtyard in peace, musing on how the debate would still be raging at his Guild, *his* Guild.

Corsini headed down to the river from his new Palace, to take the Lungarno riverside route home, humming a tune to himself as he went. He did not notice a figure following him. The man had been waiting across the street as Corsini came out of his new building, and had been following at a discreet distance ever since. He wore a billowing black cap, pulled low over his face, but apart from that looked nothing out of the ordinary in his traditional black cape.

The Lungarno was busy with pedestrians. Workers returned to their homes while wealthier Florentines started to enjoy the evening sunshine chatting casually on bridge and street corners. As Corsini neared the Ponte Vecchio, his follower sped past him on the other side of the street, still unnoticed. The mysterious man walked briskly past the entrance to the Ponte a Santa Trinità, then turned around and crossed to the river side of the street, so that he was walking directly towards Corsini.

As the two approached each other, the man took a small dagger from inside his coat and plunged it into Corsini's stomach. He did not have time to deliver a second blow as he kept on walking past.

Corsini stumbled, then fell to his knees, holding the knife which was embedded in his stomach, too shocked to make any noise. His assailant stepped calmly into a small alley that led away from the Arno, breaking into a run after twenty paces, disappearing into the early evening shadows.

A crowd quickly developed around Corsini, eager for something to gossip about when they reached their destinations. The stricken gentleman collapsed face-down, his thick dark clothes absorbing the blood as it ebbed from his body, so his injury was not at first spotted. It was only when one of the crowd bent down to help Corsini up that they noticed the dagger's silver handle protruding from his stomach as evidence of his misfortune.

One of the crowd recognised that the victim was Corsini, and swiftly realised that he would have money or possessions worth appropriating. He bent down and felt inside Corsini's robe, pulling out a purse which bulged with money. At this, the rest of the crowd forgot about the wounded aristocrat's welfare, and turned into a pack of wolves from the hills behind the City, feeding on the carcass of a fallen animal. Any hope that Corsini may have had of survival had the crowd been more benevolent evaporated as the mob gorged itself.

Within moments his clothes had been ripped off him. They were of such quality that even the strips of material would be sellable at market. When there was nothing left worth taking, he was left to die, within a couple of hundred paces of his door.

Unknown to Corsini's attacker, he himself had been followed by one of the pedestrians, an urchin who had witnessed the attack. The Signoria's desire to halt the tide of foul play was widely publicised, and the boy hoped that he might be rewarded for leading the City's police to a murderer. The pursuit wound through the narrow alleys that led away from the river, but ended abruptly when the attacker reached Piazza Santa Maria Novella and disappeared through a doorway into a palace.

The boy had no idea to whom the palace belonged, so he waited for the rest of the day to see whether anyone came out of the doorway. No-one did, and when darkness fell he headed for the Palazzo della Signoria to report what he had seen to the authorities.

CHAPTER 13

News of Corsini's murder spread through the City like wildfire. In the Benvenuti Palace, the report was received coolly – Benvenuti had not been close to Corsini, and had perceived the man as rather too traditional for his liking (little did he know of the revolution that Corsini had been trying to spark at the Arte della Lana).

Chiara knew that Donato had been 'found' by the dead man. She could see at the dinner table that night that the young artist was in considerable pain at the loss. His sorrow caused her great anguish, and she realised that the episode in the chapel that afternoon meant that she must feel some kind of love for him.

That night she lay awake, and when she knew that the whole household would be asleep, she came silently to Donato's room and slipped straight into his bed. The room was faintly lit by moonlight streaming through the thick iron bars at the window. As Donato opened his mouth to speak, Chiara placed her index finger over his lips to hush him. She reached her other arm around him and pulled his body tight to hers.

Donato had not had any sexual experience before, and immediately became hard at the close physical contact with the object of his desire. Chiara was similarly inexperienced, and wondered what it was that was poking her in the midriff. She reached down and grabbed his hardness through his hose, and he let out a sigh of pleasure. They both shook like leaves in the autumn wind.

Consumed with the excitement of the moment, they made rudimentary love, short but sweet, guided only by instinct. Afterwards, Chiara held Donato tight to her for a short while, without a word being spoken by either of them, and then returned, unseen, to her room.

When Donato awoke the following morning, he at first wondered whether he had dreamt the encounter, but he could smell Chiara's sweet odour in his bed, and knew that it had been real. As the family gathered for breakfast, Donato expected Chiara to ignore him, but instead she gave him a smile and wished him good morning as usual. Donato could not be sure whether Chiara was pretending that nothing had happened or whether her smile was unusually sweet suggesting that last night was not the end of things.

He did not find the opportunity to engage her in conversation to investigate, as a commotion arose at the main door to the palace. Captain Giannini and six guardsmen brusquely entered the dining room and addressed Benvenuti. "Sir, my apologies for disturbing you, but we wish to search your palace."

Benvenuti exploded with rage at having his breakfast disturbed without explanation, and spewed expletives at the officials. Giannini retained his calm, and suggested they move to Benvenuti's office. Once there, he explained that they had been led to the palace by the boy who had witnessed Corsini's murder. The boy claimed to have seen the murderer enter Benvenuti's palace.

"Nonsense!" exclaimed Benvenuti. "No-one in my house would ever do such a thing."

"Nevertheless," insisted Giannini courteously, "I regret that we must make a full search of the palace in order to eliminate your household from our investigations. If you do not allow us to do so, I will return with an order from the Signoria compelling you to open your doors to us."

Benvenuti had no desire for his name to be raised at the Signoria in this context so he reluctantly acquiesced to the policeman's demand.

They started the search in the servant's quarters, so that if any evidence were found implicating one of Benvenuti's staff, as seemed most likely, Benvenuti would be spared the embarrassment of having his own family's rooms searched. Nothing was revealed, however, so the search continued to the main part of the palace, starting with the smaller rooms at the top of the building.

When they came to Donato's room, one of the guards recognised the lion design brooch which Corsini wore whenever he was seen around the City, due to the lion being one of the emblems of the City of Florence. No-one knew that he had given the brooch to Donato for completing the decoration at Corsini's new palace. The heavy brooch was solid gold and therefore highly valuable, and Corsini had been murdered as he returned home from the election at Arte della Lana's Guild Hall, where he was likely to have been wearing the item. The guard instantly concluded that the occupant of the room must have mugged Corsini for the piece.

He reported his finding to Scalieri, who found out from Benvenuti that the room was occupied by Donato, and that he would by now be at work in the chapel. The guardsmen proceeded there and arrested him, to the protests of Benvenuti. Donato knew that he had done nothing wrong and so went quietly to the central prison, *Le Stinche*, for interrogation. He would not have gone so peacefully had he known the nature of the interrogation.

At the Benvenuti Palace, Chiara, who knew that Donato would be subjected to extreme treatment, pleaded with her father to intervene in her undeclared suitor's fate, which she knew would surely be death otherwise. Benvenuti ignored her pleas. He said it was better not to draw attention to his household by raising an objection to the arrest. Better instead to let sleeping dogs lie and young artists die. As a matter of fact Benvenuti doubted whether Donato was even capable of the act of which he had been accused – from what he had seen the boy was virtuous and would not bite the hand that had effectively put him in his current position. But Benvenuti would keep those thoughts to himself.

CHAPTER 14

While Donato was being led away from the Benvenuti palace towards *Le Stinche*, the final stones were being removed to create a hole hewn in the outside wall of the *Opera della Basilica di Santa Maria del Fiore*, the cathedral workshop where all the craftsmen responsible for decorating and maintaining the great building did their off-site work.

It had taken all week to make the opening, as the wall was more than 2 braccie thick, and made of solid stone. The impromptu doorway measured 5 braccie across and more than twice as high, and a substantial scaffold had to be built around it to prevent the wall from falling down.

Once the demolition debris had been cleared away, a huge contraption started to be moved towards the hole from the workshop inside. The machine and its occupant, which protruded from the top, stood precisely ten braccie high. It was swathed in thick white sheets so that whatever was inside could not be seen. It was no secret, however, that what lay beneath those sheets was six tonnes of white marble. The marble was held in a web of leather straps within a purpose-built frame made from the strongest oak.

The cradle was moved over a series of logs – the log at the back being taken out and replaced at the front as the cradle moved forward, pulled on a pair ropes hauled by teams of two dozen men each. Due to the weight of the marble inside, it could not be allowed to build up any momentum, as that would risk pulling the frame over, smashing the marble. Progress was therefore torturously slow. It took all afternoon just to move the object through the opening to the outside world.

A crowd had gathered between the workshop and the back of the cathedral, to gawp at this heavyweight ghost taking its first steps. They all knew that underneath the sheets stood the figure of David, which Michelangelo had been working on behind that wall for more than three years. Some of the crowd supported the idea, others despised it. The haters were the more vocal group, as always, and they started to throw stones at the giant as soon as it was clear of the protective walls that had encased it during its gestation.

The reasons for their disapproval were various. The statue of David was the first major artistic commission by the City since the days of the Medici. There were many citizens, mostly erstwhile supporters of the late Mad Monk Savonarola, who thought that this kind of largesse had no place in a city that had been ravaged by war and famine.

It was widely understood that the statue of David was allegorical – it represented the small City of Florence, defiant against whatever the rest of Europe (most notably France and the larger states of Italy) could throw against her. This kind of nationalism also grated with the austere introspection of the Savonarola camp.

Although the overthrow of the Savonarola regime had been greeted with joy by the majority of the City, his legacy lived on for a significant and vociferous part of the population. This group strongly believed that Florence should be less expansive. The City had become rich through centuries of trade, and their thesis was that all wealth should be put to good use in providing for the poor of the City rather than being dedicated to the territorial, academic and cultural imperialism that had characterised the Medici generations.

It was a crucial part of Savonarola's doctrine that items of beauty or entertainment corrupted the soul. He had therefore instituted a campaign of destruction, culminating in the Bonfire of the Vanities in the Piazza della Signoria, through which the world was deprived of hundreds of works of art and literature. He had appointed an army of youths, dressed in white robes, to rip jewellery from passers-by and to invade the City's homes in search of illegal objects, all of which would be removed and placed on the frequent bonfires. Although their white robes were supposed to indicate purity, members of the youth army were highly intimidating, and never slow to resort to violence to achieve their ends.

The City had been gripped by Savonarola's preachings in the years before he rose to power, to the point that, when he assumed the mantle of government, his message was distributed and enforced with fanaticism. While most of the City had rebounded gratefully from that, there were still thousands who remained convinced by his teachings of humility and modest living.

The troop of fifty men moving David in his cradle stopped work when night fell, and the crowd dispersed. They had managed to move it all of 5 braccie beyond the wall. It would be a slow journey for David to the Piazza della Signoria. The statue was to be positioned outside the entrance to the Palazzo della Signoria, within a flying spark's distance from the very spot where Savonarola had started his bonfires, the same spot where he met his own fate on the final bonfire to be built for him.

At midnight, the City was silent. Three grey shapes approached the motionless giant. One of them climbed to the top of the wooden frame to stand head to head with the hidden hero. He carried a satchel, from which he pulled six posters, a brush and a pot of paste. He poured the entire contents of the pot over David's head, and spread it around, working it into the sheets so that it would hopefully stick to the marble and be as difficult as possible to remove. He then applied the posters on to the paste.

The posters, which he and his two companions had written that day, were covered with insults aimed at the City, its government and the statue itself. It would become a familiar cycle during David's three week trip to the Piazza della Signoria – at night slogans would be attached, in the morning crowds would gather to read them with a mix of disgust and amusement before they were removed by the workmen charged with shifting the statue.

Sometimes stones were thrown at David's head too. In addition to the deep sadness he felt when he was told about this, Michelangelo wondered whether the stone-throwing was intentional irony on the part of the throwers given the legend of their target, or just blind ignorance. He decided that the latter was more likely, but it gave him no comfort.

CHAPTER 15

A messenger had immediately been sent to inform Machiavelli of Donato's arrest and the incriminating evidence. The politician arrived at *Le Stinche* shortly after Donato to supervise his interrogation personally. Donato tried to explain to the guards in the prison's central courtyard that he had recently arrived from Lucca and had been engaged by Benvenuti to paint his new chapel after painting for Corsini. He told them how he only had reasons to be grateful to Corsini for his successful start to life in Florence, and that the brooch had been a gift from the old man. The guards paid him no attention.

Machiavelli, however, listened carefully. He realised that this was the boy whom Soderini had mentioned to him after the Corsini dinner – possibly the City's next great artist. Although not a particularly senior political figure, Machiavelli had been at the dinner, since he was married to Corsini's daughter Marietta. He had not made the acquaintance of the young artist that evening, but it seemed to him a little unlikely that, having only just arrived in the City and secured a commission from one of its richest citizens, the boy would risk it all by mugging and killing his first patron.

He did not let on that he knew who Donato was, however, and ordered him to be left in chains for a day and a night in one of the overcrowded cells of the prison.

Neither did Machiavelli let on that Corsini had been his father-in-law, preferring to keep that personal element of the investigation to himself. Although, like Benvenuti, he doubted that the boy was a murderer, he did feel that if he were allowed to stew for a while his imagination would be likely to get the better of him. So terrified would the lad be of what punishments might lay in store from him (it was known far and wide that criminals were severely dealt with in Florence) that he might confess to at least something or provide some useful information before the interrogation began in earnest.

Donato endured a torrid time in the cell. The room was dark, but his artist's eye tried to measure it up as soon as he was thrown in. From what he could see, it was about eight braccie by ten. The floor was raised except for a channel through the middle down which the guards could walk. There was a gap between the raised floor and the ceiling of only half a man's height, meaning that the only way to move around the cell was on all fours.

The room was perhaps big enough for twenty men, but there must have been three times that number in there. The air was fetid, as the only openings to the outside world were two holes through the thick wall, each barely more than the size of an outstretched hand. Once the door was shut behind him, the room was almost pitch-black. Donato crawled over a tangle of limbs as he tried to find some space, provoking curses and kicks.

Under him he felt damp straw, and the reason for that dampness became clear to him as soon as he breathed in – the stench of excrement and urine was overpowering.

Donato found a small patch of filthy floor to sit on, with a pillar that he could lean against. Time passed immeasurably slowly. Nobody spoke to him other than the occasional insult. Eventually the two pin-holes of light in the wall faded as evening fell outside. But he did not sleep a wink due to a combination of trepidation at what would befall him, physical discomfort and the anguished groans of his fellow prisoners which carried on throughout the night.

Guards came into the cell at first light to wake all those prisoners that had managed to sleep. In the scant light that came into the room, and with his eyes now fully adjusted to the darkness, it became apparent that two men had died in the night. Donato suspected that this was not uncommon.

Once their corpses had been removed, Donato was taken out of the cell to the prison's torture room. He had not eaten since his interrupted breakfast the previous day, but he felt no hunger now due to the smells of cell which lingered in his nose.

His wrists were tied behind him and he was shown the Strappado scaffold. Donato knew he had an alibi for the murder of which he was being accused – he had been in the chapel with Chiara at the time. However, she had been without her chaperone and he resolved himself not to reveal their presence together, as to do so would require her to be called in for questioning. He was sure that Chiara would crumble under that pressure and reveal all the facts of their tentative relationship, resulting in catastrophe for the girl. She would at best be severely beaten by her father, a thought that Donato could not bear. At worst, she might be disowned and cast out on the street.

A guard attached him to the Strappado's rope and started to wind up the winch. Donato felt his shoulders tightening as his hands were pulled upwards behind his back. He stood on tip-toe to try to save himself from pain. But as soon as his feet left the ground and the intense pain hit his arms and shoulders, his resolve deserted him.

"It wasn't me. I was with Chiara Benvenuti, ask her, she'll vouch for me."

"That's bullshit" hissed his inquisitor, hoisting him higher. "A golden brooch in the shape of a lion was found in your room. Everybody's seen Corsini wearing that. It's obvious that it was you who robbed him."

"No," pleaded Donato. "Messer Corsini gave me the brooch because I helped with the decoration of his new palace for no wages."

Machiavelli looked on. His extensive experience of distinguishing fact from fiction in the interrogation chamber told him that this was a genuine plea. "Stop, bring him down to just above floor level. I will investigate this claim."

It would have been easy for Machiavelli to allow Donato to take the blame for Corsini's murder and face the consequences – death without trial, and case closed. The evidence was damning. But he had been charged by Gonfaloniere Soderini with solving the City's crime-wave, and he felt sure that the murder was part of that. He also owed it to his wife and late father-in-law to be certain of the culprit before closing the investigation with an execution.

He had used the previous day to investigate Donato's assertion to the prison guards that the brooch had already been in the boy's possession before Corsini's demise. On leaving *Le Stinche* he had immediately gone to speak to Captain Giannini. Giannini could not believe that Machiavelli doubted the evidence that had been put before him, but agreed to order some of his policemen to go down to the river to round up the usual malingerers there and find out whether any of them had either participated in or at least seen any of the attack on the dying man.

The policemen found strips of Corsini's clothing on two of the men who they'd found loitering in their usual places by the Ponte a Santa Trinità, who immediately regretted not getting rid of it more quickly. While administering the expected beating (there was no point taking them into custody for what they saw as a relatively minor misdemeanour), the policemen questioned the men about what they had seen.

They reported back to Captain Giannini that, although the men were highly likely to have been under the influence of wine, as was their habit, they had independently given identical accounts of the event. They were both petty thieves, using the proceeds of that activity to fund their habit, and were used to eying up the potential value of targets as they walked about the City. Their observation skills could therefore be relied upon at least to some extent. They each confirmed that, when they had seen Corsini walking along the Lungarno immediately before the attack, he was not wearing anything so conspicuous as a large gold brooch, lion-shaped or otherwise.

After Donato's preliminary interrogation, Machiavelli strode back from *Le Stinche* to the Palazzo della Signoria. A message from Captain Giannini relaying the results of his investigation into the brooch was waiting for him there. He then mounted a waiting horse and rode at a gentle trot to Benvenuti's palace, not in any rush to release the young man from his pain. The evidence of a couple of drunk criminals did not carry much weight.

When he arrived, Benvenuti himself was not at the palace, so Machiavelli was able to insist on entering and speaking to Chiara with minimal objection from the palace servants. Machiavelli was known as a cunning and quietly ruthless enforcer of the law, and they held him in considerable awe and fear.

Chiara was reluctant to meet Machiavelli, knowing that her father would not approve of her being involved in any way with the investigation. However, the man's powers of persuasion were, like his investigative skills, well honed. Within moments he was sitting calmly with the girl in the palace's impressive library.

Chiara called a servant to bring them some wine. It was considered polite to offer important guests wine rather than water, regardless of the time of day. Before aqueducts had been installed by the Medici to bring fresh water to the City from springs in its surrounding hills, wine had been the only safe drink. It could not be infected with any of the myriad diseases that dwelt in water pulled from the Arno, polluted as it was by the citizens' daily routines.

Once the servant was gone, Machiavelli issued a

simple threat that he calculated was all that would be required on one so young and inexperienced.

"I have been informed that you were with the young artist who is painting your father's chapel at the time Messer Corsini was murdered. You must confirm precisely where you were, and what you were doing. If you do not, I will tell your father that you slept with the boy. In return for full your co-operation, I can confirm that I will tell your father nothing of what you say to me. Be warned, I will know whether you are telling me the truth or not, and you must tell me nothing but the whole truth."

Her confession to something as serious as having a liaison with a man at her tender age, out of wedlock, would confirm for him Donato's innocence once and for all. There would then be no further need for her evidence. The promise not to reveal the information to anyone else was only partially genuine though. While Machiavelli had no specific plans to use the information for any other purpose for the time being, it would be stored in his encyclopaedic memory for later use should the need arise, most likely in order to effect blackmail against her father.

Chiara knew of Machiavelli's reputation as a supreme interrogator. She had never told a lie in her life, and was terrifyingly certain that he would see straight through any attempt to conceal her passionate encounter with Donato, shameful as it may be. She immediately concluded that it would be better for her and her family if she admitted her sin – Machiavelli had given his word that he would not use the information further if she came clean. If he detected a lie, she knew that Machiavelli would not hesitate to tell her father, nor to sow the seed of her indiscretion among society's gossipers, resulting in total ruin for herself and quite probably her father too. She did not consider the implications of her decision for Donato.

Machiavelli's reasoning, as usual, paid dividends. Chiara confirmed, through a stream of tears and sobs, that she had been with Donato that afternoon, and even gave up the information that they had had a more passionate encounter that night. She swore it was her first time and she would not do it again, imploring Machiavelli not to tell a soul, but he was already on his way back to his horse as her fragile voice cracked down the corridor behind him.

Riding back to the government palace, he reflected that he was just a little jealous of Donato. Chiara was a beautiful young creature. Maybe he would use the information that he had just elicited to compel her to lay with him in the same way that she had done with the artist.

Although Machiavelli's pinched face, austere hair style and intimidating persona did not make him the most attractive man in Florence, and he had only been married for a couple of years, he took any chance that cropped up to sow his seed. He blamed his promiscuity on what he called a 'conjugal famine' imposed by his straight-laced wife Marietta. The last occasion, he recalled, was one morning the previous month, in a village he had stayed in on the way to a diplomatic mission in Bologna. An old crone, who had laundered his shirt the night before, had invited him into her house before the Florentine entourage left the village. "Come in sir, I have some fine new shirts that I think you will wish to purchase when you see them," she entreated.

On entering the gloomy house, he realised he had been tricked, as the only linen on view was a towel which covered the head and face of a younger woman seated in the corner, who was otherwise unclothed. "You should try this shirt on for size, and you can pay afterwards if you like it" entreated the crone. It wasn't a bad-looking body, and appeared to be clean. Never one to judge the teeth of a horse given as a gift, as the saying went, Machiavelli took the opportunity presented by what he presumed to be the crone's daughter. He sent the old woman out of her house, lowered his hose and entered the hole that lay there waiting, without word or emotion.

Machiavelli now remembered with a grimace the moment afterwards when he lifted a piece of burning wood from the hearth, removed the cover from the woman's head and saw the ugliest young hag imaginable, with foul breath to match her looks. It had been such a shock that Machiavelli threw up all over the unfortunate woman and ran out of the house without leaving so much as the smallest coin.

He brought his mind's eye back to a much more pleasing picture of Chiara and became aroused at the thought of her lissome naked body under his. All too soon he had to revert to the real world and dismount as his horse pulled up at *Le Stinche*. He would save those thoughts for another day.

Donato was still hanging, managing to support himself a little on his tip-toes but still in searing pain too. The guard had gone to attend to other duties, knowing that Donato would not be able to escape. Machiavelli walked over to the winch and released it, allowing Donato to crash painfully but gratefully to the stone floor. He cried out as his knees hit the stone. Machiavelli smiled but said nothing, happy to have caused discomfort to Chiara's lover.

"You must leave this City and never return. If you are found in the City after today, you will be killed," he said to Donato as he marched the boy to the gates of the prison. He had no reason to expel the boy other than hoping that expulsion might improve his own prospects of conquering Chiara. It occurred to him that if he could form a patrician relationship with the girl, and that included not spilling the beans to her father about her affair with Donato, she might grow close to him and might eventually fall for his whiles. Machiavelli may have had a brilliant political and intellectual mind, but he was totally naïve when it came to affairs of the heart rather than affairs of the state.

Donato assumed that Machiavelli had informed Chiara's father of their relationship, which would surely make him a marked man. He did not know why Machiavelli was being so generous as to give him the chance to escape the City with his life, but he could not leave Chiara now. He ran painfully from the prison straight to the river, crossed over the Ponte Vecchio, and sought out Anziani's house.

Anziani was out working, but his wife Grazia let Donato in, as she could see that the poor boy was in distress. He explained breathlessly to her that he had come from an interrogation by Machiavelli after being falsely accused of murder, and that the alibi he had had to give was likely to result in him being a murder target himself. He was too ashamed to give details of the alibi, but Grazia had grown to like the boy in the time he had lodged with them, and trusted him totally. She was a sensitive woman, and could see that Donato had been through enough today already, so she did not try to pry further.

Instead, she told him to go up the ladder and rest on their straw mattress. She noticed heavy bruising on his wrists and guessed that the interrogation had been physical, so she set a fire to heat some water. When it was warm she poured some out into a cup and mixed it with some lemon juice and fresh honey from her father's bee hives just outside the City walls. She took the cup and the rest of the water in the pot up to the bed.

Once she had got Donato to drink the contents of the cup, Grazia lifted Donato's shirt over his head and saw, as she had suspected, that his shoulders were severely bruised from the s*trappado*. She told him to lay down on his front and then gently rubbed his back with a cloth dipped in the warm water. Her tender touch sent Donato to sleep.

During his earlier stay with the family, she had reflected many times that he was about the same age as her son with Anziani would have been had he survived the traumas of a complicated childbirth. She never told Donato this, but it was no surprise that she felt maternal towards the young man.

Grazia and her husband were happy for Donato to stay with them. Donato did not venture out for nearly three weeks while his strained joints recovered. By the end of that time he hoped that, without any sightings of him, it would be assumed that he had fled the City as commanded by Machiavelli and he would be forgotten about.

CHAPTER 16

The man responsible for the majority of the night-time attacks on David as the statue lumbered slowly through the streets towards its destination was Gianluca Galeazzo, the self-made cloth magnate and bastard son of the fifth Duke of Milan. He was in his late forties, and had arrived in Florence from his home town in the year 1490, just as the Medici star was starting to wane and Savonarola's was on the rise.

Once he arrived in the City, a mixture of crime and commerce brought him to prominence. His arrival was precipitated by being told by his younger half-brother Giovan Galeazzo Sforza, the sixth Duke of Milan, that he must leave the dukedom and never return. Giovan Sforza had inherited the dukedom at the age of just seven, on his father's assassination. The region had then been ruled by committee until the new Duke reached the age of twenty, and upon attaining that age the Duke wanted to put his stamp of authority on his subjects.

One of the ways that he chose to make his mark was to expel any possible threats to his power, including Gianluca, his illegitimate but older half-brother. Gianluca was not just a potential threat to Sforza's power due to his superior age and common paternity, but he had also slept with Sforza's younger sister Bianca Maria, Gianluca's half-sister, when she was seventeen. At least this was not the scandal it might have been, as she was already a widow. Bianca had been married to her first cousin, Philibert I, Duke of Savoy, at the age of twenty-one months. Philibert died in 1482, rendering her husbandless once more at the age of ten. However, a dalliance with her illegitimate half-brother could seriously damage her chances of a valuable re-marriage.

The Sforza family had managed to suppress the story from being circulated throughout the gossip grapevines of Europe, where it would have caused much amusement. But to eradicate the risk of any repeats of the incident, the newly potent Duke ruled that Gianluca Galeazzo should leave Milan without a ducat to his name.

Having known nothing other than a life of luxury as the son, albeit illegitimate, of the fifth Duke of one of the richest states on the Italian peninsular, Galeazzo had no idea of what he might do. After a heavy drinking session on the night of his expulsion, he decided to start walking south and see where the road took him. He had only reached the outskirts of Milan when, in the half-light just before dawn, he came across a merchant loading cloth from his house on to a cart to take to market in the city centre that morning. Apart from the ragged horse harnessed to the cart, no other soul stirred at that hour.

Galeazzo, still under a degree of influence from the copious drafts of wine that he had consumed that night, decided that the opportunity was too good to pass up. He silently drew the sword that the young Duke had allowed him to keep for his own safety on his journey from Milan. He crept up behind the merchant as he placed another bundle of cloth on his already laden cart, and severed his head clean from its body in a single blow as the man turned back towards his house, before the merchant had a chance to raise any cry of alarm.

Galeazzo leapt up on to the seat at the front of the cart and drove the horse forward. Knowing that he could not be seen at the market in Milan, or anywhere else in the Duchy which spread as far as Parma, he carried on south. As he sobered up in the cold first light of day, he resolved to head for a republic, which he hoped would not be afflicted by the same power-hungry bigots as a duchy.

He had heard that the Republic of Florence was, under the reign of the Medici, one of the most permissive regimes in the region. He figured that this meant he would get a fair opportunity to make some money and raise himself back to a position of influence, while enjoying whatever pleasures might take his fancy. So he passed straight through the Duchy of Modena, and on to the growing City by the Arno.

His suppositions were proved right. In 1490, the City welcomed all comers, especially those with a cargo to trade. He arrived early one morning, a week after leaving Milan. Galeazzo enquired of some relaxed guards at the City gate as to where he could find the nearest cloth market, and was amiably directed to the *Mercato Nuovo*.

There, he found the foreman of the market and agreed that, in return for letting him take a bench in the worst corner of the square, Galeazzo would give the foreman ten percent of his takings that day rather than the usual small flat fee. The foreman saw the quality of the fine northern cloth, and was happy to take the risk, especially considering that no-one else would dream of occupying that bench or paying so much for the dubious pleasure. The market was so vibrant that Galeazzo sold all his cloths by lunch-time.

Having found out how easy it was to make money with stolen goods, he thought it best not to steal from his new customers. So once a week he ventured out on raids to procure more stock from other prosperous cities lying within reach of Florence, such as Arrezzo, Siena, Volterra and Lucca. He soon had enough cash to buy a house in the City.

After a year of trading in other people's cloth Galeazzo sensibly decided that, before his wrongdoings caught up with him, he should consolidate his growing fortune by going straight. He opened an account with the bank run by the Albizzi, one of the Medici family's bitterest commercial rivals. A hundred and fifty years before, the Albizzi had been more powerful than the Medici, but gradually their fortunes had slumped.

It was a deliberate choice by Galeazzo to deposit his funds with a rival of the Medici clan. He could see that it was the Medici's turn to lose power. Galeazzo had unsurprisingly developed an anti-establishment attitude, and particularly resented the excesses of the Florentine aristocracy that he'd seen in his first year in the City. This was part of what he'd hoped to avoid in a republic, so he would do anything he could to hasten their downfall.

Galeazzo was not a particularly religious man when he arrived in Florence, but he could see that Savonarola's gospel of modest living was gaining in popularity, so he joined the monk's growing band of supporters.

More from a desire to be seen to be doing the right thing than from personal conviction, when Savonarola took power Galeazzo was one of the first to throw his recently formed collection of paintings and books on to the Bonfire of Vanities in the Piazza della Signoria. A tear came to his eye as he did it, but he blamed that on the smoke. Like many other of Savonarola's wealthier acolytes, though, he did not dispose of any of the funds he held in the Albizzi's bank, safe in the knowledge that a crucial platform on which the City's banking pre-eminence was built was the secrecy afforded to patrons.

As a result of his early and apparently positive action, combined with his growing trading success, Galeazzo quickly came to Savonarola's attention and moved up the ranks of the monk's confidants. Enjoying the rise to political prominence, he began to be swayed by the religious arguments he was subjected to and, within six months, was a fervent and outspoken believer in the power of God.

But soon Savonarola's regime started to expose itself as open to corruption, and Galeazzo once again swung away from the newly established order. Rather than being closely and openly associated with the administration by holding a role in government, he preferred to be seen by Savonarola to be contributing through his cloth trade. He made substantial donations to Savonarola's coffers, which were used for good causes around the City and preserved his good standing. He also quietly continued to amass his own fortune. Consequently, Galeazzo was largely able to escape the vicious backlash when the population recoiled against Savonarola's oppression.

Instead he could carry on with his trade as normal, albeit that many other traders refused to deal with him due to his past associations. There were enough merchants who still held Savonarola's preachings dear to their hearts for Galeazzo to continue to build his empire. He started taking over smaller cloth businesses, either by buying them or sabotaging them (murder or blackmail were his usual methods), and eventually held so much of the market that his detractors were forced to deal with him, whether they liked his politics or not.

In this way, he developed considerable power, initially in the cloth trade, and latterly at a more political level as an opponent of the governing regime. He also developed a reputation for ruthlessness, based primarily on his business methods.

Outwardly, he appeared the model of modest living, eschewing fine velvet clothing for sack-cloth, and still living in the relatively humble house that he had first bought with his ill-gotten gains. With the memories of Savonarola's cultural and social atrocities fading, Galeazzo started to be more open about his apparent religious beliefs. In part as an attempt to allay his ill reputation, he became a major donor to the hospitals run by the Cistercian, Carthusian and Dominican monks.

Many felt that the religious and social convictions which Galeazzo now wore on his sleeve were highly hypocritical given the way in which he had acted to consolidate his own power base. It was that very power base, though, which prevented anyone from voicing criticism publicly.

Galeazzo himself had no inhibitions against voicing his concerns about the way in which the City was being run. He was still strongly anti-establishment. Added to that, he vehemently upheld Savonarola's view that, rather than seeking to expand the City's commercial, political or military empire, its leaders should concentrate on improving the lot of its ordinary residents, the large majority of whom lived in poverty despite its apparent financial prowess. So he had a variety of reasons to object to the City's commissioning of the extravagant statue of David, and all that the statue symbolised.

The people of Florence did not know that Galeazzo hailed from an aristocratic background. He revealed it to no-one, knowing that it would appear at odds with his current political beliefs. Despite his name, nobody made the connection with his ancestor, Galeazzo Maria Sforza, the fifth Duke of Milan.

Before leaving Milan with his stolen bounty, Galeazzo had spent his substantial income as the Duke's first son on the traditional Italian vices of wine, women and art. He had been an early patron of Leonardo when the artist first arrived in Milan from Tuscany. This gave him another motive for disliking the colossal statue that was about to put the upstart Michelangelo at the top of the artistic tree and topple Leonardo from the position he had held there for so many years.

On Leonardo's return to Florence at the turn of

the century, Galeazzo immediately reacquainted himself with the great man, housing the artist for his first few months in return for a sketch. They were now firm friends and shared nostalgic tales of Milan, which they vastly preferred to a Florence that had become sterile since the departure of the Medici.

Like Galeazzo, Leonardo had been forced to leave Milan, for a combination of reasons. His patrons were growing tired of advancing him money for commissions that never materialised and there was talk of him being bankrupt. His promiscuous life-style was also affecting his reputation, and new commissions had virtually dried up. They felt like kindred spirits.

* * * * *

Gonfaloniere Soderini had little doubt in his own mind that it was Galeazzo who was behind the night-time attacks on David. Galeazzo had long been outspoken and vehement in his criticism of the commissioning of the statue. Like so many others in Florence, however, Soderini did not want to confront the Milanese man without strong evidence, for fear of the risk of retribution. Although Soderini was the political leader of the City, he never felt beyond the reach of violent reprisals, and his power was far from absolute. He also strongly suspected that Galeazzo was behind the rest of the crime wave in Florence, which continued unabated.

One morning he asked Machiavelli to walk with him from the Palazzo della Signoria to the river and then down to the lawns of Ognisanti at the western edge of the

City.

"Have you made any progress with the Corsini murder?" Soderini enquired.

"Very little, Gonfaloniere," admitted Machiavelli. "We thought we had the culprit, but he had a cast-iron alibi, so we've had to start again. All our investigations lead to closed doors." Machiavelli did not inform Soderini that the released suspect was none other than the young artist next to whom the Gonfaloniere had sat at Corsini's dinner.

"Have you considered Galeazzo?" asked the Gonfaloniere.

"Naturally, and Benvenuti too. But their power is so great that they can totally block our enquiries. Everyone we talk to is too scared to tell us what they know, for fear of the consequences."

"But word would never get back to either of them," protested Soderini.

"That's what I tell them, but we both know that so many of our staff are under the protection of those families that it's almost certain that information about our investigations would get through. I wouldn't talk to us if I were in their position." Machiavelli was in an uncharacteristically sympathetic mood.

"So who do you think is behind it?" Soderini continued to probe.

"Gonfaloniere, I regret to say that I still don't know. My money, for what it's worth, is on Galeazzo. I have never trusted him. I have conducted extensive investigations into him, and have found out from my sources in Milan that before becoming a rich businessman here he was a nobleman there.

"He was apparently forced to leave in disgrace, although I have not discovered the real reason. He was even being hunted there for the murder of a cloth dealer whose cart was stolen. Legend has it that he arrived in this City with just a cloth cart to his name, and my guess is that his fortune and power are built on stolen goods."

"That hardly makes him the prime suspect."

Machiavelli continued "There is evidence from his banking records that his dishonesty continued on a large scale well after his arrival here. My nephew is a clerk with the Albizzi bank and I have had him checking the records there."

"Niccolò, you know that our banks must retain their code of secrecy. Without that, we would be unable to attract investments from the Pope, the King of England and all the other rulers with money to hide. You cannot just flout it for your own needs." Soderini was furious at Machiavelli's admission that he was looking behind the veil that protected all account-holders with the great Florentine banks. It was largely the trust in that secrecy, developed over three hundred years despite the general instability of the City, which had led to Florence being one of the world's most important cities. Without the money attracted into the City, it would not be the cultural centre that it had become either.

CHAPTER 17

After three weeks of strong yet gentle cajoling along his route from the cathedral workshops to the Piazza della Signoria, and suffering nightly abuse, David was finally ready to be put in his place outside the main door of the government palace.

The statue's position had only been decided after protracted debates between the City's council and a number of its leading artists, and was still a sensitive issue for Michelangelo. Some of the artists on the positioning committee, and Leonardo in particular, had wanted to hide the statue away in an indoors location, but Michelangelo had insisted that a work of this stature should be outside for all citizens to see.

Having eventually conceded that the statue should be positioned in the Piazza della Signoria, the positioning committee then suggested that David's genitalia should be covered with a belt of fig-leaves made from copper. Michelangelo blew his top at this, pointing out that no statue from antiquity was covered in such a way and that David must be entirely bare to reveal his very soul. After all, did not the Book of Samuel proclaim that the hero had shed all his armour before his fight with Goliath? Following such arguments, the unveiling of the statue was a nervous time for its creator.

The team of labourers shunted the enormous bulk into a position that Michelangelo was happy with in order to be lifted into its permanent place. Most of them then stood back to wait and see the object of their efforts when it was finally unveiled.

Before the final part of his journey, the giant had to be freed from the cradle in which he had slumbered in the past weeks. Leather straps were fastened all around his body and attached to ropes which in turn led to three wooden cranes placed in a triangle around his intended spot. The sheets were left on the statue to provide at least some protection against the possibility of an accident, but the straps that had held him in place inside the cradle were now cut. The wooden frame surrounding him was then carefully dismantled, to leave David standing just on its base.

Oxen turned the winches of each crane, and David jerked a few inches into the air. The six tonnes of white marble immediately started to swing. The shift in weight tipped one of the cranes off its back feet, despite the piles of sandbags that had been placed on a platform at the back of each machine as ballast. The crowd that had assembled in the Piazza to enjoy the spectacle gasped as they saw the top of the crane lurch forward. Half a dozen of the watching workmen ran to jump on to the listing crane's platform as it threatened to topple over.

Michelangelo, until now observing in nervous silence biting his nails, shouted furious obscenities at the foreman, urging him to take more care. If the statue fell now, its own weight would cause it to smash into a thousand pieces.

The weight of the workmen stabilised the tilting crane, and more of them jumped on to its platform to bring its rear feet back to earth, but this only caused the statue itself to swing further in the opposite direction, like a huge pendulum. Other labourers rushed forward to the statue to try to dampen its movement. Two were knocked clean off their feet when its massive marble base smashed into their legs. The men cried out in anguish as they looked down to see their splintered bones.

Eventually, amid anguished cries of instruction from Michelangelo, to the accompaniment of more gasps from the audience, the men managed to bring the giant under control. With additional bodies now sitting on each crane's platform, and the statue surrounded by workmen to prevent any unwanted lateral movement, he was hoisted up to the level of his pediment and then gently manoeuvred into place. The straps were removed. Michelangelo erected ladders around the statue and climbed up to remove the sheets. This was not an easy process, as the paste that had been used to attach the posters had set thick. He had to use a hammer and chisel to remove much of it.

It became clear, however, that the paste had fortuitously done David a service. Michelangelo's biggest worry had been that the stones that pelted his statue every night would have damaged it, but instead the paste had absorbed the blows and protected the marble. The sculptor ordered buckets of soapy water and sponges to be brought so that he could wash the remnants of paste from David's skin.

When he was happy, he gave an uncharacteristic wave to the crowd, which by now filled much of the square, to indicate that his work was complete. A great cheer went up. Michelangelo blushed as he descended the ladder, and even permitted himself a proud smile when he turned to face the onlookers. Gonfaloniere Soderini, who stood proudly at the front of the crowd in full ceremonial regalia to celebrate the unveiling, strode forward to congratulate the artist.

He gave Michelangelo a warm embrace. Soderini looked up over the other man's shoulder at the grand statue and remarked "You have created the most amazing statue the world has ever seen. It is so great that from this angle, David's nose looks as big as Goliath's." He intended the comment to be a humorous compliment to the size of the statue as a whole, but in the excitement of the moment he had made a rare mistake. Soderini had not allowed for Michelangelo's short temper and the trauma that the artist had been through while the decision was made where to place the statue, followed by its difficult journey across the centre of the City and its nearly calamitous final positioning.

Something inside the great artist snapped. His smile instantly disappeared, and his body stiffened in Soderini's arms. He took a step back, grabbed the hammer that he had been using to chip away the paste, and charged back up the ladder that stood in front of David. "So you don't like his nose, Gonfaloniere?" he shouted from the top. "Is this better?" Michelangelo's face was red once again, and he swiped at David's nose with the hammer, taking two thirds of it clean off.

Michelangelo jumped down from the ladder in a blind fury and ran off through the crowds back to his house.

A few yards behind where Soderini had been left standing aghast at the effect of his innocent comment, Donato stood staring in awe at the statue. Anziani had told him that Michelangelo's work would be unveiled today, and he could keep himself in hiding no longer. He just had to venture out to see the masterpiece, regardless of the risk.

Donato had heard Soderini's words, and agreed wholeheartedly that this must be the most incredible statue ever carved. Certainly it was the greatest piece of art he had ever seen, surpassing anything he had seen in Lucca, and even all the works of Donatello that were scattered liberally around Florence.

"If I am ever to be a great artist, I must work with this man, so that I can learn how he can create such miracles," Donato said to himself. He resolved that, even though he had had a taste of working independently, he would offer his services to Michelangelo to be his apprentice.

Donato scrambled forward through the throng to pick up the chunk of marble that had previously sat in the middle of David's face and which now lay forlornly on the ground at the edge of the crowd. Nobody even noticed, as everyone talked animatedly to each other, or even to no-one, about what they had just witnessed. The piece of stone was almost the size of Donato's hand. He quickly left the throng before anyone else started to look for it.

As he walked back to Anziani's house, Donato congratulated himself on his good fortune. The nose would give him the perfect excuse for visiting Michelangelo. Its return might even create a sense of gratitude, although from what Donato had seen of Michelangelo's temperament, both today and on his previous encounter near Ponte a Santa Trinità, he was not sure whether the man would be capable of such an emotion.

As soon as he got into the house, he wrote up the day's events in his new diary. He was sad to have lost the original version, left hidden under his bed in Benvenuti's palace.

CHAPTER 18

The crowd ignored the fact that David's face was now missing an important feature. Florentines were never slow to take an opportunity to celebrate, and they honoured the statue's successful installation long into the night. The mobile wine-sellers, who dispensed wine from barrels on wheels into leathern, wooden or pewter tankards that citizens habitually carried with them on such days, made a fortune.

Soderini, however, returned to his office in the Palazzo as soon as it was politic to do so. He mused that the government palace's position at David's back could be likened to that of the Israelite army, and that the crowd in the square were the philistines. He had a meeting with Machiavelli planned for the early evening, to catch up on the investigation into the City's recent outbreak of lawlessness – would they be any closer to finding the Goliath causing the malaise?

Machiavelli, usually obsessively punctual, arrived a

few minutes late for the meeting, looking hot and flustered. He explained to the Gonfaloniere that he had just fought his way through the crowd in the Piazza having come from the interrogation of suspects in *Le Stinche*.

"Well that must be good news, if you have so many suspects that you are late for a meeting for the first time in your life," Soderini remarked hopefully.

"Alas, we are not much further forward. We have identified that Galeazzo has been paying for youths to throw stones at David on his journey here, as we have caught a few of them in the act and their story has been consistent.

"But I can't connect the fairly innocuous throwing of stones at an inanimate object, however important David may be, to the more serious crimes against the actual people of this City. Invariably, the stone-throwers state that they were told only to throw stones at the statue, and no matter how much we torture them, they don't appear to have any other story to tell.

"Gonfaloniere, you will have heard that all the major families, almost without exemption, have suffered some form of transgression or other. The crimes range from the theft of valuables and arson to physical violence, rape and even killing. It's been going on for weeks now, and has been so well covered up that I have only the barest of ideas as to who may be behind it all."

"What about the murder of my good friend Messer Corsini?" asked Soderini. "You arrested a young artist for that, did you not? Has he confessed? Or did he not survive your interrogation techniques? I can imagine that you would have been particularly vigorous in your hunt for the killer of your father-in-law." There was a barb to Soderini's questioning, which put Machiavelli on edge, but he continued calmly.

"He was just a lad, who I have established with absolute certainty was not at the scene of the crime at the time in question."

"Are you sure?" pressed Soderini. "I heard that he was found with Corsini's golden brooch – surely that's the strongest evidence that he robbed the man and killed him in the process." Soderini had been looking into the investigation for himself, and had discovered that the suspect was the youngster he had met at the Corsini evening.

Machiavelli suddenly encountered a rare moment of self-doubt – had he been right to believe the boy? Was Donato's influence over young Chiara so strong that he had forced her into providing an alibi despite knowing the effect that it would have on her life were it to be revealed? No, there was no way that her reaction could have been a performance – it was absolutely real. Machiavelli quickly recovered his composure. His assessment of characters was always accurate, and he knew that Donato was neither a thief nor a murderer.

"Yes, I am sure. He gave me an alibi, which I cannot currently reveal to you, but which would result in his certain death if it were to become publicly known. And I have verified its truth with an independent source whose integrity is beyond question."

"Nevertheless, I would like to question the boy myself."

"I'm afraid that won't be possible. During the

course of our interrogation, he admitted gaining illicit entry to the City, so I sent him away."

Soderini started to lose his patience. "Then who the hell do you think is behind it? All you've told me so far is who doesn't have anything to do with it. I am running out of time to get things back in order, and therefore so are you. Questions are being asked by the Signoria about whether we have control of the City." The implication was that if Soderini and his advisers did not have control, then they would soon find themselves out of their jobs, regardless of the Gonfaloniere's lifetime appointment.

"Sir," Machiavelli started, deciding it was appropriate for him to be more respectful now than he was accustomed to being, "this is the work of an aspiring prince, someone who wants to assume rule of our City, and who is prepared to go to any length to achieve that goal. He is not afraid to inflict serious injury on its people, as their fear of him is the best way to achieve their compliance with his will. He believes that the end will justify the means by which he gets there, however repellent those means may be.

"In order to achieve such a position, someone would need an abundance of three attributes: money, connections and ambition. And it is the last of these, ambition, which is the most important of them all. A prince needs ambition to drive him to be ruthless, to succeed at all costs. Without it, he will only get so far. I have given this considerable thought, and in my view there are only two people with sufficient designs on power, along with the necessary money and existing connections."

"Pray tell me who those are."

"The first is obvious – as I've said previously, the

Medici. It is well known that they wish to make a return to the City now that the legacy of Savonarola is buried. Since they have been in Rome they have been building a new power-base there until the time is ripe for them to come back here. If they can embarrass your leadership, then the City will cry out for their return. This would explain not just the crime wave but also the idiocy perpetrated in this very building for the Duke of Ferrara's visit."

"That makes sense, but who is the other?"

"Gianluca Galeazzo. As I told you before, he built his commercial empire on the proceeds of crime, and through further investigation I have uncovered the full extent of his lawlessness. Not only was he a common thief, but when people have got too close to knowing the truth about him they have a tendency to disappear.

"Although he distanced himself from Savonarola in the monk's later years, I believe he is still a religious zealot who would want to see a return to that kind of regime. And we all know that religion can drive people in ways that nothing else can."

"Then I want you to accelerate your investigation Niccolò. I know that you have made it one of your priorities to find your father-in-law's killer, and that is probably mixed up in this whole thing, but I want your action stepped up generally. We must bring the City back to order.

"The current criminal climate will be highly off-putting for investors. From being the pinnacle of European civilisation, we are fast becoming its laughing-stock, particularly with the Duke of Ferrara no doubt spreading muck about his experience here. We cannot afford for this to go on for any longer."

"Yes, Gonfaloniere, I will dedicate myself fully to the investigation with immediate effect. Rest assured that I will spend all my time on this until the mysteries are solved," Machiavelli responded with bravado.

* * * * *

Even as Machiavelli accused Galeazzo in Soderini's chamber, the man from Milan was alone in his library, figuring out how he could inflict further injury to David and maybe even Michelangelo himself. After several glasses of wine, he had worked himself up into a frenzy, and resolved that damage to the statue alone was not enough. He knew that Michelangelo had been invited to compete for another major civic project – a second great Florentine Battle to be painted in the grand hall of the Palazzo della Signoria, alongside the one that had already been commissioned from Leonardo.

The possibility that Michelangelo's Battle painting might eclipse that of his old friend filled Galeazzo with further loathing for the younger artist. While he knew that Leonardo's painting would be rendered with sympathy to the suffering of the vanquished, Michelangelo's style was likely to result in something much more imperialistic. It would glorify death and suffering inflicted in the furtherance of one city's interests against another's. He formulated a plan to be rid of the irksome artist.

CHAPTER 19

Silvio climbed up the hill to San Miniato church. It brought back memories of the disastrous escapade that had led to the loss of his older brother. The twelve year old had spent a few days sheltering in the monastery at San Marco, but soon tired of the daily tasks he was set, such as scrubbing all the floors, to earn his keep.

So he left the protection of San Marco, and since then had been sleeping in whatever quiet corners he could find. By day, he aimlessly wandered the streets of the City, lost without his brother. Stealing food from market stalls had initially been easy, but the stall-holders soon began to recognise him and chase him away before he had a chance to lay his hands on anything edible.

Silvio was now starving and desperate. While he did not want to return to San Miniato, he recalled that the Prior had told his brother that he could always secure work for them if they wanted it. He waited behind a tree until he saw the Prior come around the corner of the Bishop's palace to approach the main door of the church. He then ran and threw himself at the priest's feet.

At first the Prior was nervous about the boy's presence. He knew that the older brother had been caught and killed, and that the younger one had disappeared. He was worried that this might be a set-up, that the lad was now in the pay of the City police and would entrap the Prior somehow. He grabbed Silvio firmly by the arms and forced him to stand up. On seeing the emaciated state that the boy was now in, he knew that he must be on the run.

"What brings you here, my boy?" the Prior asked with as much sympathy as he could muster to counteract his natural caution.

"My brother is dead thanks to you. I have no family, no food and nowhere to stay," Silvio babbled.

"Then you must come with me," said the Prior, anxious not to be seen speaking to the boy, just in case anyone might be able to link him to the events that had led to Marco's death. Still holding Silvio tightly by the arm, the Prior scurried to the Priory door next to the church, checking all around him as he went, and whisked the waif in.

As soon as they were away from prying eyes, all semblance of sympathy disappeared and the Prior had to fight the urge to strike Silvio. "How dare you come here in full view of all the world? The authorities are bound to be still looking for you and you could have just led them to me."

Once again Silvio collapsed at the Prior's feet, snivelling his apology. The Prior softened a little, and this time stood him up more gently. "Ok, you can stay here for a short while so long as you pull your weight. If you want me to protect you, your will have to do exactly as I say at all times, and you are not to leave San Miniato unless I command it. Understood?"

"Thank you Sir, thank you. I'll do anything you ask." Silvio's attitude to menial tasks had been changed by life on the streets since his brief stay at San Marco.

The Prior was about to set Silvio to work when he was interrupted by a loud knock at the Priory door. He shooed the boy into a store room at the back of the building before returning to answer his caller, who was impatiently banging again at the door.

Silvio could hear a heated discussion taking place in the entrance hall to the Priory, but was not able to make out any of the content as the voices were muffled by the doors in between. It became evident that the Prior was not happy with the outcome of the conversation, as he slammed the door behind the leaving visitor then thumped back down the corridor back to Silvio.

As the Prior came through the store room door, Silvio looked up at him enquiringly. Finally the Prior's temper got the better of him and he gave the boy a backhanded slap across his left cheek, so hard that Silvio was knocked sideways to the floor. The boy looked up with a cut to his face from the jewelled rings that adorned the Prior's hand. He cowered for fear of further blows, but instead the Prior shouted at him to get out of his sight.

Silvio ran out through the rear door of the Priory, which led straight into the church. He hoped that perhaps the Prior would calm down, and in an effort to achieve that, Silvio found a broom and started to sweep the church floor.

The church remained deserted all day, isolated on top of its hill. Later, the Prior entered and found Silvio still hard at work. He grabbed the boy by the ear and pulled him back into the Priory. Noting on the way how well the church had been swept, he decided to take mercy on Silvio.

"This will be your room," he said, showing the boy to a disused *pulaio*, an indoors chicken shed. It still smelt of chicken shit, but there was a pile of clean straw in one corner for a bed. The Prior shoved Silvio in and locked the door behind him. Silvio noticed a couple of air-bricks that let in the faintest light and a little fresh air. The Prior returned with two buckets, one containing a loaf of bread, the other full of water, then left again without any further word, locking the door again.

Silvio sat on the straw and cried for the first time since he had lost his mother at the age of five. Despite his ravenous hunger, he could only nibble at the bread, but he gulped down a load of water, then promptly fell asleep, too exhausted to think any more about the situation in which he found himself.

CHAPTER 20

A few days later, Michelangelo arrived at San Miniato al Monte church early in the morning for an interview with the Prior. He had received a message only the previous afternoon that the Prior was holding a competition for the award of a commission to re-paint the ancient crypt of his church and that one of the competitors had pulled out.

Michelangelo greatly preferred sculpture to painting. The third dimension allowed a real connection to be made between the artist and his work. It also allowed a much truer representation of the subject, both physically and emotionally. The sheer effort required to carve the figure out of an immense block of stone, to release the personality inside from captivity, made Michelangelo feel that the resulting sculpture was a part of him.

Painting, by contrast, he saw as simply applying paints to a surface – there was no bond of sweat, and often blood, between the artist and the art as there was with sculpture. He often remarked that for some artists the act of painting could be likened to a spring day in the countryside, whereas for him, creating a sculpture was like the *tramontana* wind howling down a valley from the mountaintops.

On the other hand, painting did not drain him in the same way that sculpture did, so it could provide some welcome recovery time between sculpture projects. And Michelangelo was exhausted in every sense after three years of investing himself totally in the creation of David. So while he considered the decoration of a small and dingy crypt in a church outside the City walls somewhat beneath him, at this precise moment it was a job that suited him perfectly, and he was keen to win the competition.

The Prior showed him first to the crypt to be painted, in which Marco and Silvio had hidden after stealing the Caesar bust and golden plate from the Pitti. Michelangelo's jaw dropped when he saw the frescoes that were already there. "You cannot ask anyone to paint over this, it is from the school of Giotto, and it looks like it may even be from the hand of the artist himself, or if not him then that of his greatest pupil Taddeo Gaddi."

Michelangelo credited Giotto with the birth of modern painting, and had studied both his and Gaddi's work extensively in his early years under the guidance of the Medici, particularly several chapels that they had decorated in the church of Santa Croce. Neither Michelangelo nor anyone else in Florence had known that either of the artists had also worked up in San Miniato, as the painting here was cruder than the Santa Croce chapels and the crypt at San Miniato was not usually accessible, but Michelangelo could tell instantly that this was from the same school.

"As you probably know, Messer Buonarroti, this crypt is the oldest part of my church, and therefore the oldest site of Christianity in this City. So, although it may appear unprepossessing, do not underestimate its significance.

"Yes, and these paintings are of great significance too. Do you not understand that you cannot simply paint over history? If you attempt to do so, I will raise the matter with the Signoria, who will soon put a stop to it." Michelangelo once again felt his blood starting to heat up, and forced himself to calm down.

The Prior continued as if the artist had not spoken, almost with an air of arrogance. "One of our City's leading houses, who recognises the importance of this part of the building, is sponsoring the re-decoration of these frescoes. I cannot tell you who, because they have asked to remain anonymous, but if you try to prevent their will from being done, you may regret it. Such is their importance and wealth that I have little doubt that the Signoria will be persuaded not to stand in their way. And if you don't want to do the work yourself, we have three other artists who would jump at the chance," the Prior bluffed assuredly.

"I only invited you here because the patron was so impressed with your David that when Messer Filipepi dropped out of the running, he wanted you to be given the chance to bid here. Personally, I couldn't care less who does the work."

"So the little barrel Filipepi didn't want to deface the work either. Mind you, he's an old man, a commission on this scale is probably beyond him now." Michelangelo was falling for the Prior's ruse.

He thought quickly about the problem, and decided that if such great art had to be abused, then he would rather it was covered up with his own quality than some other painter's mediocrity. At least he could pay proper homage to the older work in his own, whereas anyone else would be too ignorant to do so.

"Very well, I'll do it. Are there any specific instructions?"

"None other than that the Calimala Guild should be glorified."

"So this is someone who made his fortune in cloth. That's easy to cover. Cloths of gold and purple will form a border of drapes around the ceiling of the crypt, while I shall retain the current subject and depict the dinner at Cana, with plenty of guests, including Jesus about to turn water into wine, clothed in rich robes. I'll situate the dinner in the Guild's own banquet hall."

Michelangelo let his imagination talk to the Prior of its own accord as he enthusiastically visualised the details of the completed work.

The Prior awarded him the commission on the spot. The money, two hundred florins, was acceptable. The artist didn't question why the Prior had given no consideration to the other artists who had presumably submitted much more detailed plans. Such was his ego that he had gone into the church assuming that he would come out with the contract. Even though he considered sculpture his forte, he also held no doubt that he was the finest painter of his generation.

Michelangelo said he would start work immediately

at the beginning of the following week. As he left, a young lad brushed past him on his way into the church. Able to switch from content to antisocial in an instant, Michelangelo shouted a profanity at the boy, which was as water off a duck's back.

Silvio carried on down the nave of the church.

"Do you know who that was?" asked the Prior of him.

"No idea," replied the boy.

"That was Michelangelo Buonarroti, one of the greatest artists the world has ever seen. For all his skills with a paintbrush or chisel, it seems that he has made enemies. I hear he has a rather brusque character and is quick to lose his temper."

'Like someone else around here' thought Silvio.

"Come with me," insisted the Prior, leading the young thief back to the Priory so that there was no chance of anybody hearing the instructions he was about to give.

Once he was assured of privacy, he continued with a leering smile that made his puffy mouth look even more lascivious than usual. "I have just awarded Buonarroti a commission to repaint the crypt. The poor fool is so full of himself that he doesn't realise that he's walking straight into a trap."

"What trap?" asked Silvio, eager to at least appear interested in what the Prior had to say rather than incur his wrath.

"You are going to kill him, my boy." The Prior laughed in an exaggerated manner at the contrast between the simplicity of his statement and its drastic implications for a great man.

Silvio's heart sank. "M...m...me?" he stammered. "How? And why?"

"Why is not your concern. It is sufficient that I am telling you that you are to do it. As for how, it will be easy. When he starts work in the crypt, you will be hiding in the choir-stall above its entrance. On a signal from me as he leaves the crypt for some reason, you will drop a block of masonry on his head. The church has enough loose stones following the earthquake a few years ago to make it look like a tragic accident."

"But I don't want to kill anyone," objected Silvio without thinking. As soon as the words were out of his mouth he regretted them, anticipating a violent reprisal.

Instead the Prior calmly concluded "You have no choice. If you do not do it, I will hand you over to the authorities. They will be very pleased to have caught the second brother, and they will certainly not believe your word over mine about any of this. And the way I see it, you have nowhere else to go, otherwise you would never have come back here in the first place. But just to be safe, I'm going to keep you locked up until you have done it."

With that, the Prior grabbed Silvio by the hair and threw him back into the chicken coop. He thought about giving the boy a good buggering, but decided to save that little treat to himself for later, perhaps when the plan had been successfully accomplished.

The Prior's visitor on the day of Silvio's arrival had been Galeazzo's secretary, who passed on Galeazzo's order and plan for the murder of Michelangelo. The Prior rubbed his hands in self-satisfaction at the ease with which he would be able to execute the plan, and the artist.

CHAPTER 21

On Monday morning, before Michelangelo arrived to start his preparations, the Prior sent Silvio to hide in the choir which sat atop the crypt so that he could be ready to carry out the assassination plan at the first opportunity. Much of the stonework around the edge of the choir was indeed still loose after the earthquake that had destroyed the bell-tower, ready for the boy to push over on to the unsuspecting artist.

Together they had already identified a loose slab of masonry that stood directly above the most trodden route across the wide steps down to the crypt, and the Prior had furnished Silvio with an iron bar with which to lever it over the edge.

Instead of Michelangelo's keenly anticipated arrival, however, a runner came to the church with a message to say that the artist regretted that he was now unavailable for a few months. The Prior, furious at the frustration of his plan and the embarrassment it would cause him, dismissed the messenger with a heavy kick to the backside.

The reason for such an immediate and inconvenient indisposition, not that it was given to the Prior, was that on the Saturday, Michelangelo had received a much better offer. It had taken Federico Benvenuti a little while to recover from the shock of losing Donato, his great hope of producing the next leading artist, particularly now that the boy's first sponsor, Corsini, was out of the way. Although Benvenuti later found out through the grapevine that Donato had been exonerated in respect of Corsini's death, the arrest of someone from his household for such a public offence had caused acute embarrassment.

Benvenuti had now refocused on getting his chapel completed. Having been bitten by the unreliability of an unknown teenager, he had decided to play safe and go to the top of the art establishment. Leonardo had been his first thought, but he was aware that the great man had recently been commissioned by the Signoria to paint a grand fresco in the great Salone dei Cinquecento in the government Palazzo. Benvenuti did not want to risk his commission being pushed to the bottom of the artist's list of priorities. So he opted for the next best thing in the artistic firmament – the rising star of Michelangelo.

Benvenuti was not too upset not to be using the more established figure, as Leonardo's reputation for failing to finish his commissions preceded him - not just of the bronze equine statue in Milan but smaller projects too. It was now widely recognised that Leonardo preferred to concentrate on his own fantastic initiatives, such as inventing new machines for military use, rather than spending his time on more traditional artistic commissions.

Michelangelo was a much safer bet. Still keen to prove himself in Florence having returned from Rome at the beginning of the century, there should be no question of him leaving a work unfinished. There was the added bonus that he would be cheaper too.

Michelangelo had initially resisted Benvenuti's invitation. "I am sorry, but I have only just accepted an offer from the Prior of San Miniato to paint the crypt there. I am a man of honour, unlike some other artists I could mention, and I keep to my word and to my contracts."

However, as soon as Benvenuti's dropped six hundred florins on to the table, his honour was bought out. Although there would be a little more work than the San Miniato project, this was thrice the money he'd been offered by the Prior. As a strong believer in God he felt a deep guilt at letting the church down. He had an equally great concern on artistic grounds – unless the Prior waited until Michelangelo came free again, he would not now be able to control what was painted over the existing historic work at San Miniato. On the other hand, he wouldn't then have to bear the guilt of covering it up either.

The Prior cursed loudly having slammed the big church door shut behind the messenger. The plan had been so straight-forward. He was going to blame the falling stonework on a minor tremor, which nobody in the City below would have been able to contradict. The church's choir-stall had been out of bounds ever since the last quake, because the structure was visibly loose, yet nobody had bothered to repair it. No-one would have doubted the possibility that stones could have fallen with such an unhappy consequence as the death of one of Florence's favourite sons. The more superstitious of the City's inhabitants would have concluded that it must have been divine retribution for some evil thought or deed committed by Michelangelo, perhaps even the defacing of his own statue of David that had been created for their benefit.

Now the Prior would have to inform his paymaster. He called Silvio down from the choir, gave him a cuff round the ear to vent some of his anger, and told him to relay the news to Galeazzo. "And come back straight away" he warned. "Don't forget what I know about you. If you do not return promptly, I will inform the authorities and you will find out what punishment they have in store for you – probably the same as whatever they did to your brother."

CHAPTER 22

Michelangelo was later than usual leaving his house that morning. Having agreed only on Saturday to paint Benvenuti's chapel, he had been in his studio preparing a few sketches to show to his new patron. Benvenuti had told him of the theme that he wanted portrayed, which had not changed from the brief that he had given to Donato.

Michelangelo had taken a brief look inside the chapel, but nothing more. His eye captured every detail of the room in an instant. As with Donato, Benvenuti asked Michelangelo whether he had seen Gozzoli's cycle of frescos in the Palazzo dei' Medici. Michelangelo was affronted at the question.

"Of course I've seen it. I was a student in the Medici's academy there, and was forced to study it for longer than I could bear to look at it. It is an inferior and offensive piece of work. The colours are gaudy and the characters are awkward and lifeless. If that is the quality of painting that you want, then I will get a fool in off the street to do it for twenty florins while I rest at home," the artist snapped.

"If you want to engage me, then you must be prepared to be dazzled by the pictures that I will produce for you – it will be as if I am painting one of the chapels of the Vatican palace. You will think that Moses is not just leading the Jews out of Egypt, but out of the very walls of your chapel, to the promised land."

Benvenuti was not used to being spoken to so brusquely, but he was encouraged by Michelangelo's bravado, and did not let the artist's lack of respect put him off.

Once Michelangelo had rolled up his sketches and tucked them into a bag with further drawing stocks, he dashed out of the house, as usual without saying goodbye to the rest of his family. He almost ran into Donato who was waiting outside to speak to him.

Anziani had, of course, told Donato that Michelangelo did not employ assistants and so there was no chance of him being taken on as a helper, but Donato was confident that he would be able to persuade the great man otherwise.

Donato's confidence in his artistic abilities was still buoyed by the favour that had been shown by Corsini and Benvenuti, even though that favour had ultimately not produced any positive results. He felt that if only he could show Michelangelo a little of his work, the star artist might be convinced.

Donato carried a fistful of sketches that he had produced from memory of some of the more illustrious members of Florentine society – Soderini, Benvenuti, Pitti and others – to show to Michelangelo. He did not include the sketches that he had done of both Michelangelo and Leonardo, knowing that Michelangelo hated his own appearance since breaking his nose in a fight as a teenager, and that the one of Leonardo would simply anger him.

"Get out of my way, you fool," Michelangelo shouted as tumbled out of his door. Donato quickly reached into a pocket and pulled out a lump of marble, about the size of his hand. Michelangelo immediately recognised it, and was confused for a moment. "What the hell are you doing with that?" The words were aggressive, but his manner was less so in his confusion as to why it should be in the hand of an untidy looking stranger outside his front door.

"Sir, it belongs to you," Donato said warily.

"I know what it bloody well is," Michelangelo replied, swiftly recovering his more usual persona. "As I already asked, what the hell are you doing with it, you vile object?"

"I thought you would want it back," was the nervous response. Donato had the feeling that dealing with Michelangelo was like approaching a dangerous guard dog – he looked ready to attack at any moment, and needed to be treated calmly but with caution.

Michelangelo grabbed David's nose and strode off without further dialogue. Donato followed. "Sir, may I talk to you for a brief moment?" he asked.

"If you have to."

"I am an artist, like you."

"Oh, I doubt very much that you are like me."

"Indeed sir, I can only dream of being like you. But

I would very much like to reach such heights one day."

"Where is this going? I am on my way to the Benvenuti palace to start a new job, and am late already. Why are you taking up my time?"

It was now Donato's turn to be confused. He was taken aback to hear that Michelangelo had taken his place in the Benvenuti chapel. It hadn't occurred to him until now that of course Benvenuti would have hired another artist to carry out the project. But he was overjoyed to hear that he had been replaced by none other than Michelangelo Buonarroti. However, he thought it best not to mention that he had been commissioned for the job first.

"Because the only way I can improve is to gain experience with the best. I implore you to take me as your apprentice, so that I can help with your work and learn from you."

"No, an apprentice would only delay me and distract me. I always work alone."

"I have some sketches here that I can show you. I hope you will see that I have potential," persisted Donato, unfurling his roll of papers.

"I'm not going to look at your rotten sketches. Now be gone." Michelangelo pushed Donato away roughly and the sketches scattered in the breeze. Michelangelo turned up a side street. A horse and cart walked between them and by the time Donato had gathered his papers together again, the great artist was nowhere to be seen.

Donato trudged disconsolately back to Anziani's house, with tears welling in his eyes.

CHAPTER 23

As soon as Silvio left Galeazzo's private office having told him how Michelangelo had inadvertently dodged the attempt on his life, the Milanese man furiously rang a silver bell on his desk to summon a servant to bring wine, and gave orders for his old friend Leonardo to be fetched. He knew that Leonardo would sympathise with his feelings.

Leonardo was a great artist, and he was avowedly pro-life. He was not given to the glorification of military action, even though, as a keen engineer, he had created many fanciful designs for novel instruments of war. His fascination with war was for its own sake, not for the sake of conquering other peoples and subjecting them to the conqueror's will. Galeazzo therefore expected, perhaps even hoped, that Leonardo would try to talk him down from plotting a fellow artist's death, even if that artist happened to be Michelangelo.

Leonardo arrived at Galeazzo's palace as the sun

reached its zenith, and the host invited him through to the dining room immediately to eat a simple lunch of cured meats and cheese, washed down with copious draughts of wine from the hills of Florence.

They started by discussing one of Leonardo's more unusual projects, the downstream diversion of the River Arno away from Pisa. This was yet another tactic in Florence's feud with its smaller neighbour, and had been dreamt up by none other than Niccolò Machiavelli. If they could deprive Pisa of water, its citizens would have to flee, leaving Florence free to take it over and put the river back to its original course.

Machiavelli had already engaged Leonardo on a number of military engineering projects for the Pisan war, so he was familiar with the artist-engineer's skills in this area. To put the Arno scheme into effect, he had had no hesitation in turning to Leonardo once again, who had boasted confidently that the goal could be achieved. "It goes well, we are currently digging two canals through which the river will be taken south of its current course," explained Leonardo to Galeazzo. "Victory over both nature and Pisa will soon be ours, and without the use of arms. It was a masterstroke of Messer Machiavelli to come up with such a plan."

Conversation soon turned to the main topic on Galeazzo's mind. As the wine took its effect, they both became more vociferous in their dislike for Michelangelo and his work. "The only way that I can see a stop being put to his pompous efforts is for him to be permanently deprived of the ability to perpetrate them," slurred Galeazzo.

"You mean Buonarroti should suffer some terrible injury?" asked the rival artist jokingly.

"Or worse, something even more permanent."

Leonardo realised that his companion was not joking. "That's a possibility." He warmed to the idea of removing his biggest opponent for good from the battle for big commissions. Although there was more work available now than there had been under the Savonarola regime, really meaty contracts which could keep an artist occupied for years were still few and far between. Leonardo became even keener on the idea when Galeazzo told him that Michelangelo had just been appointed to a decent commission by Benvenuti.

"Any ideas?" asked Galeazzo, not really expecting his guest to take things forward, presuming that he would balk at such action against a fellow artist.

But Leonardo did not hesitate in offering ideas. "You might remember that when we were both in Milan, the painter Gottardo Scotti died in mysterious circumstances."

"Yes, he did a little portrait for me once. Not terribly good. It was assumed that he had a weak heart."

"Well he didn't," Leonardo continued conspiratorially. "He was poisoned."

"But how? Surely signs of poisoning would have been noticed?"

"Yes, they would normally, but there are apparently some rare poisons which can avoid detection on the body."

"Who did it?" queried Galeazzo.

"That I cannot tell you." Leonardo said this with a finality that told Galeazzo that any further inquiry would be fruitless, and he was left wondering whether this meant that Leonardo did not know, or that he had been involved.

"Ok, tell me about the poison then. Is it something that we could use in the present case?"

"As you know, many artists are members of the Guild of Doctors and Apothecaries, so that they can obtain rare pigments through apothecaries' channels. I have heard talk of a new poison called Cinnabar, from Spain, although it was used by the Chinese in ancient times. It's an ore from which Mercury is obtained, but the Spanish process it to produce crumbly blocks that look just like the ochre that painters use to make up their reds. I've been told that its dust is even more poisonous than Mercury, and is very light so it will travel instantly upon the air to be breathed by whoever is grinding it.

"So if he started to grind some ochre to make his red paint, and that ochre turned out to be Cinnabar, he would inhale enough dust to kill him. And death would not be instantaneous. I am told that it takes a few days for the victim to start to feel the effects. First he will find breathing difficult, then he will start coughing up bile and blood. He will be incapacitated, before dying a slow and painful death in a few weeks. It will look like he died from a severe and rapid attack of the Consumption. So there is little danger that any link could be found to the paints, and even less danger that his death could be traced back to us."

"But artists have assistants to grind their paints. Surely if we put this Cinnabar stuff into Buonarroti's paints, we'll just kill a lowly helper. We need to get to the horse's head, not its hooves," objected Galeazzo.

"I agree that we don't want anyone else to die in

this venture. Human life is sacred, except where the possessor of that life works evil with it. But here's the beauty," purred Leonardo. "Buonarroti is so pig-headed that he doesn't trust anybody to help him. He's the only artist I know who's stupid enough to waste his time on such menial tasks as making up his own paint. I even came across him the other day on his way back from the blacksmiths with a bag of irons to make his own chisels. He was in a foul mood."

As Leonardo pondered the apparent foolishness of his competitor, he fairly spat his words out. "He deserves to die, if only for that. How will new artists learn the trade if we do not take them into our workshops as apprentices?"

Galeazzo was keen to pull the conversation back from Leonardo's rantings and focus on the practicalities of how Buonarroti's life might be cut short in an innocent-looking manner. "Once he starts showing signs of illness, won't they be able to cure him? Some priests in this City claim the ability to cure the Consumption by the laying on of hands, although I've never seen it with my own eyes."

"No, the minute he breathes in the Cinnabar dust, the process will be irreversible, and he will die as surely as the sun and the moon rise every day to revolve around us," assured Leonardo.

"So where can we get this Cinnabar from, and how can we make sure that Buonarroti grinds some?" asked Galeazzo, now satisfied that this venture might succeed.

"You can leave the procurement to me. I know a good apothecary who won't ask what I need it for," replied Leonardo, with a menacing grin. "As to applying it, I suggest you get our target commissioned for a painting, and ensure that somehow the ochre in his paint-box is swapped for Cinnabar."

"Sounds easy enough. But then I thought I had a commission sorted out for him until that damned Benvenuti interfered" Galeazzo thought aloud. "I'll just need to get that idiotic Prior to sort out another opportunity to fix Buonarroti's paints."

CHAPTER 24

As soon as Galeazzo's secretary had left the Prior at San Miniato after relaying his master's new requirements (Galeazzo avoided meeting the Prior personally as much as possible – not just because he disliked the man intensely, but also to put distance between the two of them should ever the Prior be caught out), the Prior pulled Silvio out of his chicken coop to give his next set of instructions to the boy.

"You are now to become Michelangelo Buonarroti's servant. Although he will never accept you as an assistant for his painting, amazingly he keeps no servants. I shall tell him that, in order to speed his return to complete the bogus project on our crypt, I am providing him with your assistance around his home, so that he need spend no time on his own house-hold tasks."

"But why would he take me in if he has no-one helping him there now?"

"Buonarroti is a renowned penny-pincher. You will

be providing your services to him for free, so I have no doubt that he will accept, in order that he can concentrate on his precious work."

* * * * *

And so it turned out. The Prior caught Michelangelo leaving Benvenuti's palace after work the following evening, and thrust the service of his young thief upon the artist. At first Michelangelo refused, saying he had no need of any help in his life, but the Prior was a persuasive speaker and managed to convince him otherwise before they reached Michelangelo's house on the corner of Via dell' Anguillara and Via Bentaccordi.

Michelangelo, despite being nearly thirty years old and reasonably wealthy, still lived in a house with his father and brothers, his mother having died when he was six years old. His father was enormously proud of his son's achievements in the world of art, but that pride was almost outweighed by his disappointment that Michelangelo showed no signs of ever getting married. While it was fine for the artist to prefer the company of young men, he thought his son should by now, with his money, be living independently and supporting his own family.

Old man Buonarroti, from whom Michelangelo had inherited his stubbornness, led a simple life. He had therefore never bothered with servants even though, with the money that Michelangelo had brought in through his commissions over the past few years, they could easily have afforded some. However, his health, and particularly his eyesight, was now starting to fade as he entered his twilight years. His other sons were lazy, happy to live off their talented brother's growing income and reputation. They did not lift a finger around the house, preferring to go out drinking and womanising. So Michelangelo did not mind the idea of having some help around the house, if only for his poor father's sake.

The Buonarroti were initially cold to Silvio when he arrived shortly after sunrise the following morning. Even though he knew the purpose for which he had been placed in the household, he did everything he could to ingratiate himself with its members so that he could have a comfortable time while working there. It certainly beat being pushed around by the Prior.

Silvio knew all the cleaning tasks and how to execute them from his brief stay with the monks at San Marco, and he went about his work much more diligently now. Within a few days he had cleaned the house from top to bottom, which was no mean feat, as the Buonarroti men were not given to living in tidiness.

Although Silvio could not go so far as to say that he enjoyed himself working here, he was grateful for the daytime respite from the Prior and for the time away from his chicken coop. Each evening, he trudged back up the hill to San Miniato with a heavy heart, dreading the abuse that he would have to endure when he reached "home", yet looking forward to his next escape in the morning. He was happy to toil away in the house at Via dell' Anguillara every day of the week, even though he received not a penny.

On his first day in the house, he had been told that he was never to go into the small studio that Michelangelo kept at home. Although the artist did not usually carry out his work at home, preferring to do it all on-site, he kept his extensive collection of sculpting and painting equipment there, and sometimes used the studio for doing preparatory drawings for whatever he was working on at the time, or just for random doodling whether in charcoal, paint or stone. He also kept his stock of raw materials in the studio.

Each evening, Silvio would report to the Prior on whatever he had found out during the day about Michelangelo's activities and habits. His report was usually either preceded or followed by a drunken beating from the Prior. When he told the Prior that Michelangelo kept the dyes from which he prepared his paints in the studio, the Prior realised that this was the chance to execute his orders.

A messenger from Leonardo had already delivered two small rough blocks of Cinnabar, wrapped in oiled parchment, each no more than half a thumb's length. The Prior now told Silvio to place these blocks amongst Michelangelo's stock of raw ochre, and to take great care not to damage the blocks while doing so. He did not care whether Silvio lived or died, but he did not want anything to go wrong with the new scheme.

Leonardo had told him that it should not take too long for Michelangelo to use the Cinnabar, as artists liked their raw ingredients to be fresh, and therefore kept only low stocks, even though the age of ores like ochre made very little difference to the quality of the paint ground out from them.

"But the master keeps the door to his studio locked at all times," objected Silvio.

Predictably, he received a cuff round the ear for this, before the Prior spelled it out to him. "Then you will either have to find the key or you will have to plant the Cinnabar when he is in his studio."

CHAPTER 25

Donato did not take Michelangelo's initial "no" for an answer. He was determined that the great man should see his work and recognise his ability. Every day for a week he went to the Via dell' Anguillara in the hope of finding a way to meet the artist. He would wait for a while directly across the street from the artist's house and then take a walk before returning to his station. He borrowed a wide-brimmed hat from Anziani, which he wore low over his face in the hope that no-one would spot that it was the same person who kept hanging around.

Donato studied Michelangelo's comings and goings, trying to establish when might be the best time to approach him. Michelangelo was supremely observant when he needed to be for his profession, but on any journey into or out of his house he was single-mindedly focused on reaching his destination, and so did not notice the young man in the hat loitering on his street.

The ground floor windows of Michelangelo's

house were uncharacteristically low. Donato was therefore able to see into some of its rooms from the street when the shutters were open, which they usually were in the cool of the morning and early evening. The rest of the day, they were firmly closed against the growingly oppressive summer heat.

Donato sometimes saw Michelangelo working in the room to the left of the entrance, and surmised that this must be the artist's studio. It appeared that nobody else was allowed into that room, as he always heard a heavy key being turned in a lock whenever Michelangelo entered and left the studio.

He frequently heard Michelangelo bossing someone around loudly, but whatever response was given was never strong enough for Donato to gather who it might be. One evening, he happened to see when he walked past that the object of Michelangelo's orders was a boy who looked about twelve. *'So he does accept some help,'* Donato thought hopefully to himself, even though it was clear that the boy did not assist with anything artistic. *'There must still be a chance that I can convince him to let me work for him.'*

Donato resolved to speak to Michelangelo again as he left his house, but he wanted to see whether he could catch the man in a slightly better mood than usual.

One morning, Michelangelo came out without his equipment bag, instead carrying an empty hessian sack with handles, but he looked as irritable as ever. Donato guessed that he must be on his way to the market to buy some provisions, and wondered whether the artist might be happier on his return.

Unlike any other Florentine, who would stop and

natter in the market with anybody they were even faintly acquainted with, Michelangelo went with the sole purpose of getting what he needed and returning home as quickly as possible. The market was crowded, and the shoppers' chatter was inane.

Before long, Donato heard the now familiar footstep of Michelangelo's nailed boots coming back towards him. He looked up and saw his target storm round the corner into Via dell' Anguillara with a bulging bag of groceries which was falling apart and spewing out fruit as he went. Michelangelo's temper seemed even darker than normal, so Donato decided once again that it was not a good time to attempt making contact, but undertook to himself that he must do so tomorrow. Otherwise, he might be waiting there for months before catching the man in better humour.

The following morning, as was more usual, Michelangelo came bounding out of the house with his equipment bag over his shoulder. Donato was waiting on the other side of the street ready to approach his target. He had his pictures unfurled to show to Michelangelo.

As he approached, Michelangelo instantly recognised Donato as the one who had accosted him there earlier in the week. He walked towards Donato to meet him in the middle of the street, which Donato took as a promising sign. But instead of waiting for Donato to show him his drawings, Michelangelo grabbed him and pushed him with considerable force back up against the wall of the building opposite his house.

"I told you once already, I do not want to see your bloody sketches, and I do not want your bloody help," he growled, just inches away from Donato's face. Donato felt Michelangelo's enormous strength. Although he was a small and wiry man, the many years he had spent bending marble to his will, both in quarries and in his studios, had given him great power.

Michelangelo drew even closer to Donato's face, so that their lips were nearly touching. He paused there, while Donato shook, before taking a step back. Donato almost whispered "Sir, I have seen that you have a boy working for you. Please just look at my pictures, and you will see that it should be me helping you. I can do everything that he does and provide assistance with your assignments."

At this, Michelangelo pushed Donato roughly to the floor. Donato's head hit the stones with such force that he fell unconscious and a trickle of blood started to flow from where contact had been made just behind his left ear. His drawings blew down the street in the wind.

Michelangelo turned his back without a care and went on his way to work as if nothing had happened.

A middle-aged woman returning home from the market stopped to study the crumpled figure on the pavement. She could see from the poor state of Donato's clothing that there would be nothing to be gained from rifling through his pockets. So instead she gave him a shake, and when there was no reaction she put a bottle of wine to his lips.

Donato came round with a start. "What's happened?" he asked, to nobody in particular. The kindly woman just said that she had found him laying there unconscious. She helped him to sit up and lean against the wall against which Michelangelo had just pinned him. Once she could see that he was ok, she continued on her way.

Donato stayed sitting there until early afternoon, still in a daze but also feeling generally sorry for himself. It was then that he saw a movement from within the house out of the corner of his eye. Michelangelo's studio was quite dark, and he did not want to be caught by the returning artist or one of his brothers overtly peering in. So he kept his position on the other side of the street, but strained his eyes to see what was happening. Although the buildings were too high to allow direct sunshine to reach the ground floor, the sun was in that direction and so the room was a little lighter than it might otherwise have been.

The movement was the slow opening of the door into the studio. He then saw the young lad who was working there enter the room cautiously and start looking around the equipment that lay there. The boy had a furtive air, but eventually seemed to find what he was looking for, as he reached into a pocket and pulled something out, which he then placed carefully in a box that sat on the main table in the middle of the studio. Donato had no idea what the boy could have planted, but thought it strange that, never having seen anybody other than Michelangelo enter the studio, this newcomer should creep in and leave something amongst Michelangelo's effects.

Donato put that little mystery out of his mind as he heard brisk footsteps approaching.

Another failure to report in the diary. His new book made fairly depressing reading so far compared with the optimistic direction of the original, which he hoped was still hidden in his old room at Benvenuti's palace.

Grazia threw Donato a disapproving look when

she saw the dried blood on the back of his head on his return to Anziani's house, but said nothing. As they chatted after their usual peasant dinner, he mentioned the oddity that he had observed in Michelangelo's studio to his host.

"Yes, it is suspicious," agreed Anziani. "I doubt very much that Buonarroti would have authorised the boy to intervene in any of his materials. He considers the handling of the tools of our trade as sacrosanct, and will not allow anyone near them. I think it stems from when the Medici were overthrown, and some zealous followers of Savonarola confiscated all his kit.

"Did you know that it is possible to kill someone by putting poison in their paint? Many artists have died over the years because of this, some accidentally, others intentionally. I can only think that someone is looking to do a mischief. These are strange times in Florence. I would keep this information under your hat for now, you never know when it might become useful."

"Stop with your ludicrous conjectures, I'm sure it was nothing, the boy was just tidying, like I always have to do after you two," interrupted Grazia. "Get yourselves to bed now, tomorrow is the feast of San Giovanni. You'll no doubt be carousing late into the night, so you need an early night tonight."

"Yes, and because it's a Friday tomorrow, with only half a day's work to be done the following day, it'll be an even heavier San Giovanni than usual," warned Anziani. "We'll first go and watch a game of *calcio* down at Santa Croce, then head for the centre and get stuck into some wine. You'll need it after you've seen the game."

CHAPTER 26

Although the feast of St John was a public holiday, so there was no work for anybody in the City apart from a skeleton staff of servants going about their usual duties, there was no chance of sleeping in. Church bells shattered the still that hung over the City in the small hours, celebrating the coming of dawn on the auspicious day with peal after peal. San Giovanni was only three days after midsummer's day, and everybody in the City was awoken early in order to pay proper respect to the baptist of Jesus in their local churches before more liberal festivities could commence.

There had been festivals throughout Italy for hundreds of years to celebrate the summer solstice, and when Christianity took hold of the region, the day of San Giovanni happily provided a perfect excuse for the retention of those celebrations. Even now, the festivities were subject to a strong pagan influence, although that had been heavily frowned upon during the Savonarola years.

Crowds poured out from their long church services, some feeling pious, others with a guilty sense of relief. They moved like herds of sheep towards the centre of the City, the Piazza della Signoria, the Piazza di San Giovanni where the Baptistery stood, and the palace-lined streets which lay between those two main squares. The busiest of those streets would be Via dei Calzaiuoli, the shoemakers' street, which ran straight along the route of an ancient Roman road. Here the revelries would carry on well into the night.

Anziani, Grazia and Donato walked from their church of San Frediano along the south side of the river as far as Ponte a Santa Trinità. Anziani remarked, for Donato's interest, that the bridge they were crossing been built by Taddeo Gaddi a hundred and fifty years ago after its previous incarnation had been washed away by the great flood of 1333.

When they reached the north bank of the Arno, they turned right to continue walking along the river towards Piazza Santa Croce. They arrived at the square, which had had its cobbles covered with a thick layer of sand and sawdust, in time for the start of the day's first game of calcio.

Donato had never witnessed anything like it. Two teams of muscular men stood opposite each other, one in bright red, the other in bright blue. At the sound of a huge drum, a ball was thrown into the middle of the square, and mayhem erupted. The teams fought each other so viciously for the ball that at first Donato had to turn away from the game. He wondered how such a cultured City could indulge in something so barbaric. But the crowd around the square shouted and cheered for their preferred team with such glee that he was compelled to continue watching.

Donato found it hard to deduce the aim of the game beyond inflicting as much pain as possible on the members of the opposing team. At some points, it seemed that the ball was deliberately thrown away at one end of the square or the other, but then the chaos was started all over again from the middle. Every so often a player was hurt so badly that he had to be taken away on a stretcher and another one took up his place, though Donato could not understand why anybody would willingly play this savage game.

He could not tell whether either team could be considered to be winning, although the fans who had started out cheering the blues seemed to be getting angrier as the game progressed. Anziani was far too wrapped up in the action to explain, while Grazia had as much idea of what was going on as Donato.

After a long while, both teams were dead on their feet. The drum that had started the game was struck again, and the team in red held their hands aloft and hugged each other in joy, while the team in blue hung their heads in shame. The crowd spilled on to the square to congratulate the red players or to remonstrate with the blues, depending on their allegiances.

The three companions then headed into the City centre, towards the Piazza di San Giovanni, which Anziani always felt was the most appropriate location for enjoying the eponymous saint's day. Anziani was happy, as the victorious reds were from a quarter to the south of the river, and it was always good, if unusual, to score a victory against the arrogant north-bankers. He belatedly explained the rules of the game to Donato in case they returned later. There would be games between different quarters of the City all day long.

Caught up in the crowd moving along the Via dell' Anguillara, Anziani was surprised to see Michelangelo Buonarroti coming out of his house with his equipment bag slung over his back. Donato shrank back, fearing another attack if Michelangelo spotted him. Anziani, who knew Michelangelo a little from the star artist's early days of learning his trade, greeted him. "Buongiorno Messer Buonarroti. I see you carry your work with you – will you not join the City in celebrating San Giovanni?" he enquired.

"Oh no. This is a perfect day for me to work – I know that everybody will be out here, so I will not be disturbed," chirped Michelangelo in an uncharacteristically happy mood.

"Then let me introduce you to my good friend Donato. He is a fine artist for one so young," said Anziani, pulling Donato forward.

"This little shit? I've met him before, and I doubt he could paint a wall white," Michelangelo almost joked.

"No, seriously," insisted Anziani. "He's a good kid."

"Well, I'll give it to him that he's persistent, which helps. Maybe I'll take a look at him."

Before they could talk further, Michelangelo was borne away by the crowd. They went their separate ways, Michelangelo towards the Benvenuti palace, the other three up Via dell'Acqua to skirt around the Piazza della Signoria on their way to the baptistery square.

They crossed over the Via della Vigna Vecchia, the 'street of the old vine'. "An appropriate street name for today, given the amount of produce of the vine that will be consumed," commented Anziani. The usually taciturn artist had become a sudden fount of information, with his excitement at the day that lay ahead.

When they finally reached the baptistery square, Donato was shocked to see that many of the old pagan gods and goddesses of legend appeared to live on. Citizens celebrated the deities of wine, fertility, the sun and moon and many others, dressed in garish and often obscene costumes.

The influence of Bacchus, the pre-Christian Roman god of wine, was particularly in evidence, as men dispensed gallons of his red liquid from barrels that they pulled around on miniature carts. Every reveller carried their tankard, the bigger the better, usually attached by a rope or chain to their belt to avoid misplacing it in an inebriated moment. They could fill up with the intoxicating refreshment for just a couple of small coins. Many had clearly been at the grape for some time, rather than paying their respects to the one true God, and were singing drunken songs or performing debauched dances all around the square.

Anziani led them to join up with his friends at their usual meeting place on this day outside the Misericordia, a charity for the poor. On a normal day here, abandoned and lost children would be on show in the loggia – if they were not claimed within three days, they would be fostered out, to a caring family if they were lucky, but more often to a life of hard labour and little love.

Donato took a few cups of wine, but his mind was elsewhere. It was the first time he had ever seen Michelangelo in anything approaching good humour, let alone being amenable to him. He had a growing feeling that he ought to make the most of it. Of course, Donato didn't have his drawings with him, but if he could get to his old room in the palace, his sketches for the very chapel that Michelangelo was now painting might just still be there. And he would dearly like to recover his first diary book if that had not been removed from under his old mattress. He was also worried about what he had seen the boy place in Michelangelo's paint box now that Anziani had told him it might be poison.

Donato knew that the Benvenuti palace would be virtually deserted. Among the crowds were plenty of servants, and Donato was sure that even most of those in the Benvenuti household would be allowed out to join in the festivities. Anziani could see that his protégé was distracted, and knew why. "Go on, get out of here," he told Donato.

While Donato fought his way westwards against the throng, which now filled all the streets leading into the square, Michelangelo was getting ready to paint his first wall. Benvenuti did not show Donato's sketches to Michelangelo, knowing that he would pay them no heed. But the supremely talented artist had taken just a few days to mock up some cartoons on Benvenuti's theme of Moses leading the Jews out of Egypt.

When Michelangelo presented them to his new patron, Benvenuti could only admire them as the work of a genius, although he did ask why Moses had horns growing out of his head on the descent from Mount Sinai.

Michelangelo had to bit his tongue to provide a civil response. "Have you not read the book of Exodus? It says that, without Moses' knowledge, God placed horns on his head to show that they had conversed."

Benvenuti was puzzled, but gave his approval to the artist on the strength of the rest of the plans. He had, of course, read Exodus and the rest of the bible, although not since his youth. He checked the passage later, and the Latin confirmed Michelangelo's depiction.

At Michelangelo's insistence, the palace staff had erected a makeshift scaffold that could be moved around the room to allow him to access the upper reaches of wall and the ceiling. The artist carefully laid out on the floor his cartoons for the first wall, which showed the Egyptian hunt for newborn Israelite boys and Moses being placed in his papyrus basket in the reeds by his mother.

He then went to his paint box and arranged a row of coarse stone pots in which he would first crush his raw dyestuffs, then stir in a little water to turn the dust to paint. He wanted the paints all ready to go before he mixed the plaster, so that he had the maximum amount of time with the plaster still wet. Any plaster that he had not finished painting over would have to be hacked off and reapplied the next morning.

CHAPTER 27

Knowing that he would not receive an open welcome to the palace, Donato went straight to the servant's entrance. From his time there, he knew that this door was often left unlocked, as servants came and went with frequent errands to keep the palace stocked with all manner of supplies or to run messages to other members of the City's elite.

Even though, as Donato had hoped, most of the servants were out enjoying the day, the door was indeed unlocked, and Donato was able to enter without hindrance. He went straight up to his old bedroom. His heart sank to see that the room had been stripped – the walls and the bed were bare. All trace of him had been removed from the room. There were no drawings left for him to show to Michelangelo. He felt nervously under the mattress, and was relieved to find that his diary had not been discovered and was still where he had left it.

Donato placed the diary in a pocket inside his tunic

and made his way back downstairs to head for the chapel where he hoped to encounter the artist at work. Without the drawings from his room, he would just have to try and persuade Michelangelo to let him demonstrate his skills by doing a drawing or painting for him.

Michelangelo opened up the box which contained his dyes in their individual drawers, including the Cinnabar which Silvio had inserted in place of the normal ochre for red. He took a sample of each colour from its drawer and placed it in one of the pots.

With a small stone pestle he then started to grind the azurite which would become a rich blue. It was a painstaking and time-consuming process, but a satisfying one too. Michelangelo trusted only himself to grind the dyestuffs to the right consistency for the paint he required – a fine dust. After a while he pursed his lips and gave a gentle puff into the mortar. A little blue-tinged cloud rose from the bowl, and he was satisfied that the powder was ready to become paint. If this were the Cinnabar, it would have been sufficient for him to inhale a fatal dose.

He added a few drops of water to the ground azurite, and stirred it gently until all the dust was absorbed and the liquid paint had the right consistency to be applied to the walls. Michelangelo moved on to a block of lead-tin oxide, which would make a bright yellow. It powdered easily, and he soon had it in its end state ready to paint with.

Donato ran down the corridor that he had walked more calmly along many times before on his way to work in the Benvenuti chapel. As he neared the door at the end of the corridor which gave on to the walled garden one side of which was occupied by the chapel, the deaf old head servant came in through the same door, having just delivered some fresh water to Michelangelo.

The servant shouted something unintelligible at the top of his voice, and grappled with Donato in the doorway. In his desperation, Donato struck the old man in the stomach and he crumpled to the ground. He hurried through the door, and onwards towards the chapel.

But the old servant's shout of distress had been heard, and brought younger servants, first one, then two more, running from their chores in the palace.

Michelangelo tried to ignore the old man's shouts as he reached once again for one of his raw dyestuffs. This time he selected the red pot. He picked up the pestle, and was just about to attack the rocks when Donato burst through the door.

The first servant already had one hand on Donato as they tumbled into the chapel, and he wrestled the younger artist to the ground, sending the scaffolding flying. It fell on to the cartoons for the north wall of the chapel. The other two servants ran in and, recognising Donato as the young lad who, they felt, was no better than them but had lorded it in the company of the Benvenuti family, the three of them proceeded to administer a thorough battering. He tumbled over the fallen scaffolding, and it crumpled under the affray. Donato tried to pull himself into as small a ball as possible to leave the minimum amount of body surface exposed to his assailants.

Michelangelo looked on in disbelief. The good mood that he had been in at the thought of a quiet day's work while the crowds swarmed in the City centre swiftly evaporated. Without a word, he stormed out of the chapel, then out of the palace and straight down to the river to avoid the jubilant crowds, leaving his materials standing where they were, unaware that he had inadvertently avoided breathing in the lethal Cinnabar dust, for now at least.

'*Fools,*' he thought to himself angrily. '*How can I be expected to function in such conditions? I will return on Monday to gather my things. Damn his money. I'll have to go back and work for that idiot of a Prior.*'

CHAPTER 28

The three young servants did not even notice Michelangelo leaving, so engrossed were they in their treatment of Donato. They eventually satisfied their thirst for violence, and decided that it would be best to call the City police to deal with the intruder before they had a corpse on their hands.

By now Donato was in some agony, and was coughing blood over Michelangelo's drawings.

One of the servants went to seek a local police guard, but being San Giovanni, he had to fight his way through the crowds all the way to *Le Stinche* before finding any officials on duty. Even then they were reluctant to get involved, until the servant revealed who his master was. The possibility of a reward for positive action, or perhaps the threat of punishment for inactivity, secured their cooperation. Benvenuti had highly placed friends everywhere, including in law enforcement.

Two guards were ordered out by Captain Giannini,

who happened to be on duty at *Le Stinche*. They trudged behind the servant. Rather than wading through the increasingly drunk and tightly knit bodies occupying the City centre, the servant decided to lead them round to the north, via the church of Santissima Annunziata. The detour only angered the guards even more.

It was mid-afternoon when they reached the Benvenuti palace, and they were little interested in noting the facts that the servants offered. It was a baking hot day, and they were nearing the end of their shift. When they got Donato out of the building, he could barely walk. The guards decided that, rather than walk the long way round again, it would be better to see how things were proceeding in the middle of the City. They could even perhaps pick up a drink on their way back to dropping their charge off at the prison, as they both carried their tankards with them in readiness.

They did not need to bind Donato's hands behind his back as they would normally have done, as he was in no fit state to escape. They merely held a shoulder each and marched him down the Via del Sole then on towards the Piazza della Signoria. This was their preferred place for the celebration of San Giovanni as it was not overhung by the religious shadow of the cathedral and baptistery, and they need therefore feel no guilt about the inevitable irreligious behaviour.

The guards barged their way straight through the square, picking up a cupful of wine each on their way. They were heading down the side of the Palazzo della Signoria when, from the *aringhiera*, the platform that ran around the Palazzo on which City dignatories took their comfortable seats on days such as this, Machiavelli spotted them from the corner of his eye.

Machiavelli did not recognise Donato, as he was crouched over in pain. But the politician was tasked with restoring law and order to the City, so when he saw somebody being led away by police in the midst of the festivities, on a day when crime levels were usually very low, it piqued his interest. He begged leave from his neighbours on the *aringhiera*, then jumped down and caught up with the trio as they crossed the Via dei Leoni.

The guards turned round in surprise when they heard a nasal upper class voice calling out to them, and they were even more startled when they saw that they were being addressed by Second Chancellor Machiavelli. He was often seen around *Le Stinche* and so was easily recognised by those who worked there.

"What have we here then, my good policemen?" he enquired.

"Sir, we bring this prisoner from the Benvenuti palace. He was caught breaking and entering – it seems that the damned foreigner is just another agent of our current crime wave. The staff there have already made him pay pretty badly though, he's not in a good way at all," laughed the older guard in response, not feeling the need to speak as formally as he usually would to the likes of Machiavelli due to the festive atmosphere all around.

Machiavelli grabbed Donato's hair to lift his head and speak to him, and was surprised to see that it was the boy who he had sent away from the City a few weeks earlier. He said nothing for the time being, as he did not want the guards to see that his order had been disobeyed. In addition to pain, Machiavelli could see a pleading in Donato's eyes – the boy knew that he was in for more pain when he arrived at *Le Stinche*.

Knowing that Donato was a promising artist, Machiavelli was curious as to how and why he had got himself into trouble again to such an extent that his life was once more in jeopardy. Machiavelli believed that Christianity had softened his fellow citizens compared with how men were in the ancient civilisations, and was growing tired of the inane celebrations going on all around him in the name of the religion. So he followed the guards to *Le Stinche* where he insisted, without giving any explanation, on taking Donato to the interrogation room that was set aside especially for senior members of the City's government and business community.

Unlike the rest of *Le Stinche*, much of which resembled a cess-pool, this room was decorated luxuriously. That served two purposes – dignatories could have all the comforts that they were used to in their own palaces, while their prisoners were lulled into a false sense that they would be treated well. In fact, this room had seen more deaths than any other in *Le Stinche*, as those same politicians and businessmen frequently used it discretely to kill off anyone who might have crossed them in some way.

Having taken several cups of wine outside the Palazzo della Signoria, although he would never take so many as to render himself in any state other than total control, Machiavelli was in benevolent mood. He remembered telling Donato that if he were found again in the City he would meet his end, but looking at the pathetic young creature before him, Machiavelli's heart softened just enough to spare him his life, for now at any rate. He invited Donato to explain what he had been doing since their last encounter.

"Sir, I am an artist," started Donato hesitantly, struggling to breath and to speak. "Both Messer Corsini, may he rest in peace, and Messer Benvenuti have considered that I have a little talent. This blessed City is the only place where I might be able to develop that talent into something greater. I am very sorry that I did not leave when you told me to, but I feel that it is my destiny to be here."

"What were you doing in the Benvenuti palace? It seems to me that you waited for a day when you thought the palace might be deserted, to sneak in perhaps to steal something. Or did you fancy that the girl might be there?"

"No sir, I have not seen her, I swear." Donato broke into a fit of coughing at the thought of Chiara. Machiavelli poured a cup of water from a flagon on the desk and held it to Donato's lips so that the boy could drink.

Recomposed, he continued, "You are right though that I saw an advantage to there being fewer staff in the palace today. I have been trying to meet Michelangelo Buonarroti to show him what I can do, without success. I saw him on his way to the palace this morning, and thought I might be able to speak to him there."

"Why did you need to break into a palace to find him? Especially when you knew you would not be welcome there. Surely it would have been easier to meet him at his house, that is not difficult to find," suggested Machiavelli.

"Believe me, sir, I have tried that. I have

approached him a couple of times, but he always seems to be in a bad mood so I have had no joy. When I saw him this morning, he was in a fine mood," explained Donato.

"Well, you seem like an honest and intelligent boy to me, even if it was foolish to ignore my command to leave the City, for which you will pay later. However, last time you were shown to be telling me the truth. As I am sure you are aware, we are in the midst of a crime wave in our dear City. You are a foreigner, and people like you will always be top of our list of suspects, so I would have no difficulty in locking you up in one of the less delightful rooms here, and soon all trace of you would be lost."

Machiavelli was interrupted by another coughing fit. This time he did not offer Donato any water, fixing him instead with a cold stare, preferring to allow the boy to be racked with pain. When the coughing eventually subsided, Machiavelli carried on.

"I want you to tell me everything that you have seen since arriving in Florence which might be out place."

"Sir, I have seen nothing at all," replied Donato, unable to turn his mind back through his time in the City. Still in a daze after his beating at the hands of Benvenuti's staff, he forgot that he carried his first diary in the pocket inside his tunic, which may have revealed something useful.

"Then, as I said, I will leave you to fester in this 'palace'. Are you sure that you can think of nothing?"

Having already spent a day and a night in one of *Le Stinche*'s main cells, Donato was fully aware that a prolonged stay here would almost certainly be the end of him. Conditions were such that it would probably be impossible for anyone to survive for more than a few weeks before starving, catching a fatal disease or being beaten to death by rival inmates or guards. He tried desperately to review his time in Florence, and replayed the last few days in his head.

"There is one thing, sir, which I thought a little odd. It's probably nothing, and if that is the case, then I apologise. There is a young boy who has just started work in the Buonarroti house. While trying to meet Messer Buonarroti, I've spent some time waiting on the other side of the street from the house and have seen through the windows some of the things that go on inside. I know that Michelangelo always keeps his studio locked so that no-one apart from him may enter. But yesterday, while he and his brothers were out, I saw this boy enter the studio and place something amongst the artist's materials. The senior Buonarroti is too old to hear or see the boy creeping around."

"You're right, that probably is nothing. But then it may be something. I'm going to keep you here. If that turns out to be useful information, then I will release you, and if not, then you'll have to give me something better. You will have plenty of time to reflect. If you think of anything else which might be useful, let the guards know."

Machiavelli went to the door and shouted for a guard to fetch Donato and throw him into one of the cells. On his way out of *Le Stinche*, he gave orders to Captain Giannini to send word to him straight away should the boy have anything to tell him.

Donato was pushed roughly into one of the cells, and was greeted for a second time by the unwelcome smells and noises there. He pulled himself into a sitting position with his back to a wall. He pulled his knees up around his ears and put his hands over his head, and gently sobbed. This was not what he had come to Florence for. From such promising beginnings, how had things come to this, he wondered, and, more importantly, would he be able to get out of this situation?

CHAPTER 29

Machiavelli immediately went to the Buonarroti house, which was only just around the corner from *Le Stinche*. Rather than going in, he spent some time observing the house from the same spot where Donato said he had stood for long periods.

The servant boy that Donato had mentioned had evidently not been allowed to join in the celebrations going on in the City centre, as after a while Machiavelli could hear Michelangelo loudly berating the child for some poorly performed cleaning task. He waited for the noise to die down, then rapped on the door.

He was let in by an old man, who he guessed must be the father of the Buonarroti brothers, and asked to see their servant.

"What is your name?" Machiavelli asked when the boy was brought in from the kitchen.

"Silvio, sir" was the timid response. In a flash, Machiavelli remembered Captain Scalieri's report on the death of the youth they had caught following the defacing of the Salone dei Cinquecento. The intruder had given up precious little information, but the report had referred to him saying that his partner in crime was his younger brother, who went by the name of Silvio.

"And how old are you?"

"Twelve, sir." So this could be the boy referred to as the intruder's brother in Scalieri's report. Maybe he was involved in more than just that petty crime, and as a young boy, Machiavelli knew that it would be easy to extract any relevant information.

"Where did you get this boy from?" Machiavelli asked, turning to Michelangelo and his father, who were standing next to the boy.

Michelangelo responded that the Prior of San Miniato had insisted that they take him as their servant, for no charge.

"Why did he do that?"

Michelangelo had managed to calm down since leaving the Benvenuti chapel. He explained how the Prior thought the boy's assistance might speed his return to the church to complete his contract, but admitted that he thought it a little odd.

"I hope you don't mind, Signori, but I am going to have to take him away for questioning." Machiavelli was the height of politeness in the company of Michelangelo, who he knew he had to treat with kid gloves if the City was going to be able to commission him at a good price for future projects. But his priority was to get to the bottom of the mystery that was opening up before him.

"No, take him away, he's a pain in the arse and I

never wanted him here anyway."

Rather than taking Silvio to the room in *Le Stinche* where he had just interviewed Donato, Machiavelli decided it would be better to take the youngster to the more imposing Palazzo della Signoria. He held the boy tightly by the arm all the way, and twice had to counter bids to escape his grip. The sun was now low in the sky. Even though the San Giovanni celebrations would carry on well into the night, it was likely that Captain Scalieri would be at the government palace, and he wanted Scalieri to be involved in questioning this boy in case he had any other knowledge from when his brother had been prisoner.

Machiavelli led Silvio through a small servants' door at the rear of the palace so that he did not have to negotiate the crowds thronging around the main entrances that he would normally use. Unfortunately for Silvio, the Captain was in the palace, and had drunk extensively from the wine-sellers in the square outside. Machiavelli looked concerned when Scalieri's intoxication became apparent, but Scalieri was alert enough to detect the worry in the second chancellor's face. "You know the old Florentine adage – 'Life is for enjoying,'" he said by way of explanation for his state.

Machiavelli seemed to accept this, and following a brief recount of his recent findings, Scalieri was delighted to take the boy off Machiavelli's hands. He would normally have taken him straight to the Strappado to force out any available information, but the wine gave him a better idea.

Scalieri hauled Silvio up the main stairs in the Palazzo della Signoria, then up several flights of much smaller stairs until they reached the level immediately below the roof. Machiavelli followed behind them.

"This will be a fine spectacle for all to see on San Giovanni," he laughed, as he leaned precariously out of a large opening in the wall to reach a rope that hung down from a wooden beam which extended from the wall into the night sky. Machiavelli thought for one horrible moment that Scalieri was going to fall out. "Anything you want to tell us about who you're working for?" as he tied the rope around Silvio's chest.

Scalieri did not even wait for an answer before pushing Silvio through the opening, to swing freely under the beam. Silvio had no head for heights and instantly wet himself. A handful of mystified revellers below looked up at the clear night sky wondering where the shower had come from. The light from the torches that blazed around the square was just enough to illuminate the source. They cheered when they saw the boy hanging like a puppet high above them. The cheer rippled through the crowd like a wave as the spectacle was noticed around the square.

"The Prior of San Miniato sent me to work for that artist," the boy shouted in abject terror at Scalieri and Machiavelli, who had followed them up to the palace's eves. Although Machiavelli knew that Scalieri was drunk, and had guessed what he had in mind the moment he set off up the stairs, he was happy to acquiesce in Scalieri's actions. "He wanted me to put some poison in Buonarroti's paint."

"I don't believe you," Scalieri shouted back. "Your brother spouted about the Prior too – what nonsense."

Just then, explosions started going off all around them. Machiavelli and Scalieri looked out to see *fuochi artificiali*, artificial fires, being launched by rockets into the sky from down below in the square. When the rockets reached their zenith just above the rooflines, they exploded, lighting up the black sky with their fire, but more impressively creating deafening bangs. It was even louder up here, nearly level with the explosions.

A massive black box, the size of a small cart, was suspended on a web of ropes that ran between the parapet of the Palazzo della Signoria and the other buildings around the square. The crowd below marvelled when it started spewing out its own exploding rockets. They saw one of the rockets land on the roof of the *Portico dei Pisani* across the square from the Palazzo, causing a fearful blaze to take hold.

The multitude roared its approval once again, particularly enjoying the fact that it should be this building that was burning. It had been built by Pisan prisoners after Florence's victory over them in the Battle of Cascina a hundred and forty years ago. Such events were etched on the minds of every Florentine, however deep in the past they may be, and the fire assumed even more significance as Florence was now at war with Pisa once again.

Pulling his attention back from the distractions outside, Machiavelli shouted to Scalieri "You said his brother talked about the Prior of San Miniato – what was that about?"

"Yes, he was obviously talking rubbish, so I didn't put it in my report, but the older boy said that the Prior had put them up to their handiwork on the walls downstairs."

"And now this one says that the same Prior was getting him to poison Michelangelo Buonarroti. Maybe there is something in this. We will go and see the Prior in the morning."

The two men climbed back down into the bowels of the palace, leaving Silvio hanging to entertain the crowd, even more terrified than he had been at first, as explosions clattered all around him and fire raged in the building opposite. When they got back to the ground floor, the reverberations of the explosions going on outside forced Machiavelli to take pity on the boy. He dispatched a guard back up the stairs to haul him in and take him to the cells.

In a further stroke of misfortune for Silvio, the guard sent to retrieve him was even more inebriated than Scalieri. He found where the boy was hanging, untied one end of the rope from a hook on the wall next to the window, and watched in surprise as the boy at the other end of the rope suddenly disappeared from view. The celebrations below were cut short for one member of the crowd as Silvio landed squarely on top of him. Amid the fireworks and intoxication, barely a soul noticed.

CHAPTER 30

On the morning after San Giovanni, the City was a mess. Street cleaners would usually be out at dawn to clear away the detritus of the previous day, but today those cleaners were delayed by hangovers, along with most of the rest of the population.

Scalieri suffered similarly – after leaving Silvio to his fate and receiving instructions from Machiavelli to meet him at San Miniato at midday, the former soldier had gone out to enjoy himself. He awoke feeling fragile but had a strong constitution and by midday was outside the church ready for action. He was uneasy about what might happen with the Prior, but happy that he would not have to make any decisions in that regard, able to leave it to Machiavelli.

When Machiavelli arrived, he told Scalieri that after leaving the palace last night, he had gone back to the *aringhiera* where a few members of the City's council remained. "I knew that Gonfaloniere Soderini would still be there, overseeing his City to the last.

"I wanted to report yesterday's progress to him, and ask whether he knew anything about this Prior. He told me that he's heard whispers that the Prior has a shady side, although he didn't know anything specific. So we are just going to arrest him now, take him down to your Strappado, and see what he can tell us."

The Prior had taken his full quota of wine, and more, the day before, and was taking advantage of not having to host a service today by trying to sleep it off even at midday. Scalieri knocked loudly on the Priory door, which was opened by a novice monk. "Where is the Prior?" the captain demanded.

The novice hesitated, knowing that to disturb his master would put him in a foul mood for the rest of the day and probably result in a good flogging.

"Come on, we haven't got all day," reinforced Machiavelli. If you don't tell me then we will search the Priory until we find him." The novice could see from Scalieri's uniform, with flamboyant plumes in its cap and the fleur de lis designs embroidered on his doublet, that he was some kind of senior government official, although he did not know who the other man was.

When Scalieri reached for the truncheon that hung from his belt, the novice decided that it would be best to accede to their demands, and led them to the Prior's chambers. Scalieri opened the door, and they found the Prior snoring loudly, spread-eagled across his bed, still wearing his robes from the previous day.

They had to shake the Prior violently and slap him round the face to rouse him from his deep slumber. He came round slowly, confused as to his whereabouts and what was happening to him. Finally he had recovered sufficient consciousness for Machiavelli to inform him that they were taking him down the hill to the Palazzo della Signoria.

"Do you have horses, as I fear my legs will not carry me?"

"Of course we don't, don't be so lazy." Machiavelli had little sympathy for the corpulent clergyman, but when they got him off the bed, they realised that it would be a struggle to get him down into the City without transport. They called to the novice, who helpfully informed them that the Priory had a horse and cart, to take produce from the garden there down to the City markets for sale to raise money for the upkeep of the estate.

Scalieri went to the stable and tethered the ropey-looking horse to the cart. The three of them, including the novice, then man-handled the Prior on to the back of the cart, where Machiavelli also jumped up to keep an eye on him. Scalieri drove the cart slowly back down the hill to the government palace.

When they got him there, Scalieri called some of his guards out to help carry the Prior into the inquisition room. As Machiavelli had privately suspected, the Prior's character was weak, and they did not need to do anything more than take him near to the Strappado for him to offer to tell everything he knew if only he could sit down. Machiavelli told a guard to fetch another seat for the Prior, which he placed immediately beneath the Strappado so that the Prior was constantly aware of the threat hanging over him. Machiavelli himself took the seat that was already behind a desk, and sent for pen and paper to take notes.

It took most of the afternoon for the Prior to recount all his wrongdoings, so extensive were they. Much of what he said was currently of no interest to Machiavelli, such as his mistreatment of a string of children who had been placed in the care of the Priory, although Machiavelli enjoyed the irony that he should be taking this confession of egregious sins from a priest.

However, when it came to the Prior's account of how he had been acting on behalf of Gianluca Galeazzo in organising many of the crimes committed around the City in recent months, Machiavelli paid particular attention.

"I believe he came to me because nobody would suspect a Prior of being behind a campaign of criminality."

"But why would a man of God, as you profess to be despite what you have already told me, agree to carry out these atrocities against our fair City?"

"Galeazzo's secretary explained to me that he knew about my weakness for children, and threatened to expose me to the Pope. I could not risk the excommunication that would certainly result from that."

"Yes," Machiavelli agreed, "Galeazzo has a wide network of informants, and I imagine you are not the only one who he has blackmailed in this way. But again I say, as a supposed man of God, should you not have turned him away when he told you to commit further wrongs?"

"It started out as nothing much, just a minor theft which I was able to bring about easily. I thought he would go away then, but he came back for more, each time with the same threat. You are right, I should have stopped it, but once I was on the wheel of sin I found I could not dismount. I was disgusted with myself, especially for ordering the rape of several fine women."

"You should be disgusted with yourself for everything you have done, not just that."

"Galeazzo also said that he would fund the reconstruction of my church's earthquake-stricken belltower. I think I tried to use this to justify my actions to myself and to God." By now, the Prior was weeping heavily.

It must have been the influence of the wine the previous day, but Machiavelli had forgotten that the reason Silvio had given for his being placed with Michelangelo was to bring about the artist's death by poison. He was so absorbed by the extent and variety of crimes that the Prior had commissioned, and with observing the man's fall from apparent grace before his very eyes, that he omitted to query whether Michelangelo was at risk.

By the time the interrogation finished, night had fallen. With the Prior locked up in one of the cells under the Palazzo della Signoria, Machiavelli was exhausted and could see that even Scalieri was flagging. He decided that it would be safe to leave the arrest of Galeazzo until the following morning after Sunday Mass.

CHAPTER 31

By the next morning, though, news had spread around the City that it was the Milanese merchant who had been responsible for the City's turmoil. One of the Signoria guards had gossiped about what he had witnessed of Galeazzo's interrogation (which was not very much) to a friend over a drink that evening, the friend told another friend, and soon the story was being posted as news.

Despite having been a follower of Savonarola, and still being deeply religious, Galeazzo was a naturally flamboyant figure, and although he did not deliberately chase fame, he could not help but attract attention. As an outsider, there was always a degree of distrust of him among Florentines. This was exacerbated by the stories, which he could not escape, about his wealth being based on those early thefts.

So when the latest revelations swept the City, its citizens were quick to jump to a mass conclusion that he must be guilty. Machiavelli could detect a mood of unrest in the City even when he walked from his home to Mass in the cathedral that morning. He passed a few posters pasted on street walls declaring "Galeazzo the criminal master" and "Milanese thief found out", and decided that it would be best not to wait until after Mass to arrest the man.

Machiavelli therefore diverted his path, without too much sadness at missing church, to the Palazzo della Signoria, where he found Captain Scalieri already on duty having been to an early Mass. He told the captain to raise a troop of six guards, and they proceeded on foot directly to Galeazzo's palace on the nearby Via delle Terme, next to the public baths just behind the *Mercato Nuovo*.

Here they found an angry mob already forming. Galeazzo had seen the start of this earlier, and had not ventured out to church, preferring to remain safe behind the mighty oak doors to his palace.

When Scalieri rapped authoritatively on the doors with his baton, one of the guards inside the palace opened a panel to see who it was. On seeing that it was an official delegation from the Signoria, he let them in with a measure of relief, thinking that they had come to protect the palace. The crowd behind had not yet turned ugly enough to seize the opportunity to surge through the opening.

Machiavelli and Scalieri wasted no time in being shown to Galeazzo, who was in the small private chapel of his palace, kneeling at the altar. Machiavelli coughed from the back of the room. When Galeazzo turned and saw him, he realised that his time was up.

He turned back to the altar, looked up at the image of Jesus on the cross, said a small prayer, crossed himself and rose. He walked resignedly to the door, where

Machiavelli explained merely that they were going to take him to the Palazzo della Signoria to question him in connection with information received from the Prior of San Miniato.

In the short time that they had been inside the palace, the crowd had swelled further, for many people received the news about Galeazzo as they left their own church services and came straight here to see whether anything interesting might develop. And they were not disappointed, as the palace's doorway was opened to reveal Galeazzo being led away in the middle of the Signoria guard.

A great jeer went up from the crowd, and many hurled abuse at Galeazzo. By now, the whole street was full of protesters, and the guards had to use all their strength to push their way through. Then the crowd started to move with the guard along Via delle Terme back towards the Signoria, and some began throwing more than mere words.

Initially, they threw marrow seeds, picked up from any street vendor as a snack on the way to or from church that morning. Then some bent down to pick up stones from the street. The guard's ceremonial uniforms and soft caps offered scant protection against such projectiles, and they tried to hurry along faster.

But more citizens now approached from the other direction, and there was no way through the seething mass of bodies. The normally mild Florentines who, only two days earlier, had filled the streets with dancing and music, had turned into a pack of hungry carnivores, and they scented a kill.

Rocks now rained down on the guards, and some

of the crowd started attacking them with punches and kicks, aimed at getting through the soldiers and finding Galeazzo, who cowered in the midst of the guards. Machiavelli and Scalieri simultaneously came to the conclusion that they would not get out of the situation with Galeazzo alive – if they and the guards were to survive, they would have to allow the angry mob to have its fulfilment.

Machiavelli assented with a nod of the head to Scalieri's unspoken question, posed by the raise of an eyebrow towards Galeazzo. Scalieri pulled his guards away one by one, leaving Galeazzo exposed to the savage will of the collective beast around him. The last they heard of him was a muffled scream as he was enveloped in a sea of pushing, shouting bodies.

Scalieri dejectedly led his troop of guards, along with Machiavelli, back to the palace. When they got there, Gonfaloniere Soderini was waiting, having received a message from Machiavelli to say that they were arresting Galeazzo. The Milanese man may not have been popular, but he was very wealthy and highly influential. Protocol demanded that his arrest be dealt with at the highest level of government.

Soderini was surprised to find that Galeazzo was not with the battered looking party that returned to the Palazzo. "Well, that at least saves us the diplomatic problem of how to deal with him in custody," he pronounced pragmatically when Galeazzo's lynching was explained to him.

"He has no family here other than his strumpet of a wife, who I anticipate will be happy to move along without too much of a fuss if she can be left with just a small portion of his assets," Soderini continued thinking aloud, as the pair walked slowly up the stairs to the Gonfaloniere's office. "We will hold a posthumous trial, and if we find him guilty of anything serious we will be able to sequester the rest of them.

"And if your information is correct, Niccolò, we will all be able to sleep much better at night, in the knowledge that, with the Prior locked up and Galeazzo dead, we will have no further disturbances in our City.

"You have worked hard on this, even ruining your day of San Giovanni, thank you. Now go home and get some rest, you've had a difficult morning. Remember that tomorrow we have a Signoria meeting at which we must discuss raising taxes, which will not be a popular proposal. However, the City is very low on funds.

"Not only do we have to fund your project to divert the Arno away from Pisa in order to win that war, but I am told that a Spanish army is advancing north from Naples with its sights set firmly on us. If we do not raise more money then we will be unable to recruit a sufficient army to defend ourselves, so I will need your rhetorical skills to be at their best."

CHAPTER 32

Machiavelli arrived at the palace just after daybreak to prepare for the meeting of the Signoria. Although he felt he had achieved considerable success with the outcome of the concluded investigation, he was not one to rest on his laurels, and Gonfaloniere Soderini had made clear yesterday that a good performance would once more be expected of him today.

And, when he thought about it, his investigation had finished positively due, in no small part, to a significant slice of luck. Had the artist boy not reappeared in front of his eyes, he would not have been led to the little thief and thence to the Prior and Galeazzo. But with Galeazzo's premature death, he now had no way of knowing for certain whether it was the cloth-merchant who had been behind Corsini's killing or not.

He had barely sat down at his desk when he was interrupted by a guard sent with a message.

"Sir, I have come from *Le Stinche*. Captain Giannini

told me to inform you that this was taken from the boy you brought in there on Saturday and that you might find it interesting." The guard handed Machiavelli a tattered looking book, with a confused look on his face, unable to understand how a small book scrawled in by a lowly prisoner could be considered interesting.

"How is the boy?" enquired Machiavelli.

"I saw him this morning, and he did not look at all well. I do not think he will see another morning. Would you like me to return a message to Captain Giannini?" He received nothing more than a wave of dismissal in return.

Machiavelli flicked the book open and realised that it was a diary. He closed it again, knowing that he should put it aside for now, in order to continue preparing the speech that the Gonfaloniere wanted him to deliver to justify asking Florence's citizens to pay more taxes. But he was curious to find out whether the diary would provide definitive vindication of his decision to release Donato in the investigation of his father-in-law's death, so he permitted himself to open it again. The handwriting was poor, and the language simple, but any writing at all was more than could reasonably be expected of a young craftsman. Although Donato had spoken well, he had clearly not been fully educated in the art of writing.

Machiavelli started to read the page where the book fell open.

Today I am confused. Messer Benvenuti is involved in something I not understand. I hear him talk to his clerk about Messer Corsini. He not say nice things. He say maledetto Corsini seen his bank transfers. I know Messer Benvenuti bank with Messer Corsini...

This must be before Corsini's death, Machiavelli thought, so he flicked forward to the final page of writing in order to work backwards. Here he found what he was looking for.

Today is very bad day. Two bad things happen today. I hear that Messer Corsini is killed. He good man, and good to me. This very bad news. I wish he still alive.

So Machiavelli had been right - Donato was certainly not the murderer, as he would not have thought to put a decoy lie in his diary.

Other thing is I kiss Chiara. Feels very good, but I know very bad. If Messer Benvenuti find out, he probably kill me. He protect her a lot. I not know what love is, but I think I love her. She look beautiful. She smell beautiful. She feel beautiful. I can only think of her, but I know this wrong. I must confess this to priest in church, confess not just kiss but my feeling too. But what if priest tell the Messer? No, priest cannot tell, I will confess.

But even now in bed I cannot think of anything apart from Chiara. She occupies me. I must try to think of something else.

I must reflect on life of Messer Corsini. He good man, to think of him is good, better than to think evil thoughts of girl. Why he killed? Who killed him?

Questions Machiavelli was keen to find definite answers to also, as his investigation had gone nowhere until the revelation concerning Galeazzo, and he still had lingering doubts that it was Galeazzo who lay behind everything. He read on.

I wonder if Messer Benvenuti involved in Messer Corsini death. This another bad thought, I cannot think it for sake of Chiara, but it keeps coming back to me when I think of Messer Corsini.

This poor boy can't stop beating himself up,

thought Machiavelli. He even felt a little remorse at the treatment that Donato had received, although he quickly absolved himself of any responsibility for that on the basis that the boy had been half-dead when he spotted him on San Giovanni, and would probably have died anyway. Plus he hadn't left the City when told by Machiavelli to do so, and had been caught breaking into Benvenuti's palace, so he had to fear severe retribution.

When Messer Benvenuti speak to his clerk about Messer Corsini, it sound like he want to do bad things to Messer Corsini. But Messer Benvenuti is good to me, and he has beautiful daughter. I cannot talk about this to anybody, as would ruin Chiara if her father in trouble. I cannot do that to her. Again my thoughts have come back to dear Chiara. I should not think any of these bad thoughts. I will stop writing now to stop these thoughts. I will go to sleep.

And there the writing finished. A sudden realisation dawned on Machiavelli that the page he had first started to read might contain something a little more interesting. He leafed back through the book until he found once again the entry for the day when Donato had overheard Benvenuti talking to his clerk.

... Messer Benvenuti say that Messer Corsini is a dangerous man, that he must be stopped from saying something, that Messer Corsini knows about transfers of much money through his bank from Messer Benvenuti to Messer Galeazzo, that these transfers are for nothing.

I am in room next to office when this talk happens, so I not hear everything clearly. I writing it down now straight after so I not forget. Messer Benvenuti I think say that if Messer Corsini knows about transfers to Messer Galeazzo, that may put Messer Benvenuti in problems. I not understand why.

Machiavelli rose, still reading, and walked to Gonfaloniere Soderini's office next-door. He knocked quietly, and was invited to enter.

"Sir, I know that we are preparing for an important conference this morning. However, I would humbly request that you break off from that for a moment to review this and give me your opinion on it. If the information that I have here is correct, then I fear that our immediate action will be needed if we are to avert the death of someone who is very dear to this City."

Soderini frowned impatiently at his advisor. "Fine, but explain it to me quickly."

"This diary was taken from a young artist currently being held in *Le Stinche*. He arrived in Florence a few months ago, and was using it to keep a record of his time here. Somehow, he was commissioned by Benvenuti to paint his chapel. He was allowed to stay in Benvenuti's palace, as a result of which there are some rather interesting diary entries."

Machiavelli read out the same two passages that he had just read to himself, and concluded "So it looks as though we may not have caught our master criminal after all. We have assumed that Galeazzo lay behind all these crimes, but what if it wasn't him? What if he was just the middle man for Benvenuti?"

"You mean you are going to take the word of some stupid boy from Lucca. We cannot arrest someone of Benvenuti's standing just on his word."

"I read this diary to say that Corsini had found out some information about payments from Benvenuti to Galeazzo which the latter did not want to risk being disclosed to anybody else. What could that information be? My only answer is that the payments must have been for something untoward. Otherwise, he would not have minded people finding out.

"If Benvenuti was behind Corsini's murder, and the boy's diary is correct that he has made more than one payment to Galeazzo, then it is a reasonable assumption that it is he who is trying to destabilise the City. Christ," it dawned on Machiavelli, "Benvenuti wants to overthrow you and the government in order to take power for himself. It is only a matter of time before our citizens become sufficiently angry at our lack of progress in tackling the crime-wave to back his demand for a change of order." Machiavelli's mind was now racing.

"*Madonna Miseria*," he exclaimed. "These pages have triggered my memory, which must have been momentarily clouded on the day of San Giovanni, that an attempt was being made on the life of Michelangelo Buonarroti."

"So if it was Benvenuti who was really leading the plot to kill Michelangelo, then our artist is in danger. He has, of course, been commissioned to paint Benvenuti's chapel – what if that is just a ruse to get him where Benvenuti can attack him?" Soderini was warming to Machiavelli's new theory.

"No, they're using poison to kill him. The snivelling little thief said the Prior wanted him to plant some poison, and that young artist from Lucca you mentioned said he saw the boy putting something mysterious among Michelangelo's painting equipment. We don't know what or where the poison is, but we've got to act quickly. We may be too late already," Machiavelli conjectured.

"Perhaps we should ask the Prior or the boy about the poison," suggested Soderini. "You do still have them in custody I trust." Machiavelli blushed at the barbed reference to his release of Donato a few weeks back which had allowed the boy to attack Michelangelo.

"Of course I still hold the Prior. But news of Galeazzo's death is bound to have reached him already, even in the cells. So there will be no reason for him to tell us the truth unless we force it out of him with physical means.

"The boy was not up to Captain Scalieri's interrogation techniques." Machiavelli did not reveal the real reason why, when he arrived at the palace after arresting the Prior, he was informed that two crumpled bodies had had to be cleared away from the pavement next to where David now stood.

"We may not have time to go and question the Prior in *Le Stinche*, where I ordered him to be moved yesterday. I sincerely advise that we should go to Messer Benvenuti's palace now sir."

Soderini paused to consider, before responding. "You, Niccolò, will not be able to just wade into Benvenuti's palace and take him away for questioning. It was different with Galeazzo, he was known to have been a crook, and he held far less influence than does Benvenuti. But we only have highly questionable evidence against Benvenuti for now. I will need to come with you for this. It will require sensitivity and respect." The risk of losing Michelangelo, and the blame that he might have to shoulder for such a loss, had evidently hit home with the senior politician.

"Gonfaloniere, if you are to remain as leader of this City for the remainder of the term of your appointment, I am certain that you will need to learn to be more ruthless," suggested Machiavelli.

"You have many skills, Niccolò, but those qualities of sensitivity and respect are not highest among them. And it will require the authority of my presence to enable you to convince Benvenuti's staff to allow him to be removed from the palace should he wish to resist.

"We will have to inform our fellow councillors that this morning's conference is to be adjourned until our return. Come, let us not waste another minute, so that we may have our meeting yet."

CHAPTER 33

Gonfaloniere Soderini left instructions with his private secretary to allow the meeting of the City's councillors to gather as normal in the Salone dei Cinquecento, as he did not want them to disperse. The hall had been whitewashed on the very day that the Ferraresi had walked in on the embarrassing scene left by the palace intruders. He told the secretary that if he and Machiavelli had not returned by the time they were all assembled, he was to inform them that the Gonfaloniere had been delayed for a short while by some urgent business, but that the meeting would proceed as soon as he returned, which was expected to be very shortly.

Meanwhile, Machiavelli went downstairs to instruct Scalieri to raise another troop of guards.

"I hope today's exercise is more successful than yesterday's," Scalieri commented snidely.

"I would be careful with that tongue, Captain. The only possible explanation for how the news that Galeazzo was wanted came to be so widely known before we went to arrest him is that it was leaked by one of your guards. And let us not forget that it was your guards who let those stupid boys into this palace to embarrass us before the delegation from Ferrara. We will be looking very carefully at you."

"Yes sir," Scalieri mumbled in a submissive tone which Machiavelli preferred. "Might I be permitted to know the nature of the current mission?"

"Did you not hear what I just said? Your guards are responsible for Galeazzo's lynching before we could question him in detail. Under no circumstances will I impart any more information than is absolutely necessary. You will follow me and the Gonfaloniere, and I will instruct you when I need to do so."

Soderini arrived outside the guardroom, in his full regalia of a bright blue cape embroidered with red fleurs de lis and a plumed cap. Machiavelli brought short swords that he had picked up from the Camera delle Arme for each of them. Soderini looked at him disapprovingly, never one to pursue violence if a diplomatic solution might be available.

"Sir," pre-empted Machiavelli, "if you wish to see your life-time appointment as Gonfaloniere through to a natural end, you really must learn that, before all else, a leader must be armed. It was a lesson that Machiavelli had learned only the previous day.

They climbed on to a pair of the horses that were kept ready for emergencies. The gate was thrown open and they cantered out, with the Scalieri still shouting orders to members of his troop to follow.

The two riders were forced to wait for a moment while the guards assembled. They then guided their horses at a brisk trot through the streets to Piazza Santa Maria Novella, with the guards running at a fair pelt behind. Scalieri, with his bad leg, struggled to keep up, but after his rebuke from Machiavelli, he made sure he was not dropped.

As they could only trot to Santa Maria Novella without losing the guards, Machiavelli took the opportunity to continue reading the diary from the saddle, while Gonfaloniere Soderini led the way. He read about the surprise that Donato had experienced when asked to paint Benvenuti's chapel, with the owner to be at the centre of the depiction, and refreshed his memory about what the young artist had seen while standing outside the Buonarroti house.

Scalieri did not have time to work out where they were heading until they arrived. Gonfaloniere Soderini and Machiavelli had already dismounted and tied their horses up to the iron rings that hung for that purpose on either side of the palace's main door, and were waiting impatiently for the guards to catch up.

Soderini could see that Machiavelli was itching to charge in, but he wanted to do things in his own calmer way. "Leave this to me please, Niccolò," he requested, and approached the door. The palace must have had a permanent look-out for visitors, because the door opened, seemingly of its own accord, before Soderini could even touch it.

The City's leader asked quietly to see the Messer Benvenuti. The footman recognised the importance of the visitor and so led the band of men slowly but directly to the anteroom outside Benvenuti's office. Another servant blocked their way into the office itself.

"My master is in a meeting sir, and cannot be disturbed," the servant explained.

Machiavelli's impatience could take no more. "You cannot speak to our Gonfaloniere like that. I don't care who your master is in a meeting with, we must see him now." With this, he brushed the servant aside, swung the door open and strode in. The scene that greeted him surprised even the unflappable Machiavelli.

CHAPTER 34

Benvenuti stood over Michelangelo, who was bent backwards on the desk with a silver dagger pressed hard to his throat.

"Nobody walks out on a contract with me for no good reason and lives to tell the tale," he shouted into the artist's bearded face, oblivious to the door having just been opened.

It was clear to both Machiavelli and Soderini who followed him into the room that Benvenuti, despite his reputation for serenity, was on the verge of killing Michelangelo. Veins stood out in blue against his puce forehead, and spittle showered down on Michelangelo's face as he shouted. The dagger was pressing into his victim's windpipe, and had already drawn a spot of blood.

"Let him go," spoke Gonfaloniere Soderini, firmly but calmly. Benvenuti flicked his eyes sideways to espy his intruders.

"No, this bastard has paid me the ultimate insult of

trying to worm out of a deal." Benvenuti was still shouting. "I will not have that. I have not reached my level of success by allowing people to back out of contracts, and just because this one's some great artist doesn't make it any different."

Captain Scalieri had by now entered the room, and he saw a chance to atone for the mistakes that Machiavelli had highlighted earlier. Benvenuti was so enraged that his eyes were watering, and he did not notice Scalieri start to move away from the doorway. He edged around the side of the room until he was entirely out of Benvenuti's field of vision towards Soderini and Machiavelli.

Soderini still tried to find a peaceful resolution. "I understand that, but killing him will not solve your problem, not this time. This man is too important for his death to be ignored."

"No Gonfaloniere, I cannot let him get one over on me. As soon as one person does, they all will." Benvenuti was virtually howling with rage. Machiavelli recognised his strange behaviour as a kind of madness he had read about in ancient Greek texts, and he knew it was dangerous. Benvenuti's mind was temporarily but totally deranged, and he could do anything in his current state, including killing Michelangelo.

"He must die," cried Benvenuti, almost in a sob, swiftly pulling back the dagger to plunge it into Michelangelo's stomach.

Scalieri had by now sidled round to the opposite side of the desk. He seized his moment with perfect timing. With remarkable agility given his bad leg, he threw himself over the desk and into Benvenuti, knocking the aggressor off Michelangelo and on to the floor. The knife clattered away across the floor, and Scalieri found himself lying on top, able to restrain Benvenuti.

Everybody in the room paused for a few moments, rooted to their spots in shock at what had just occurred. Eventually, Machiavelli tapped Scalieri on the shoulder to signal that he could move away. He and the Gonfaloniere then lifted Benvenuti to his feet. He was calm now, seemingly a different person from the monster they had just seen. They felt safe enough with him to sit him at his desk, and send Scalieri and Michelangelo out of the room, along with the guards who had ventured in to gawp at the tumult.

"Tell me what this is about, Federico," requested Gonfaloniere Soderini in as soft a voice as he could muster through the tension of the situation. "I cannot believe that you wanted to kill one of our greatest artists over a simple contract."

"I don't know, Gonfaloniere," Benvenuti replied numbly. "I have recently found myself flying into rages over the smallest of things. I, who usually am in complete command of my emotions, find that I am unable to control myself. I do not know what is happening to me."

Machiavelli looked quizzically at Soderini, as if to ask whether he could step in with some questions of his own. Soderini nodded him on, hoping that he would pursue a sympathetic line.

"Sir," he started respectfully, to Soderini's relief, "I have information to say that you have been involved in a number of crimes around the City. Is there anything you can tell us in that regard?"

To the great surprise of both Machiavelli and

Soderini, Benvenuti broke down at this. "Yes, it is too much, I cannot continue with my charade of innocence and sophistication – as you have just seen, it is not me." And so Benvenuti confessed, there and then, that it had been him behind the villainy that had afflicted the City these past months. He said that he had done it because a voice inside his head had told him that if he could disturb the City enough to make its citizens resent their current leadership, he would, through his considerable money and influence, be able to take power.

"How did you find out that it was me?" asked Benvenuti, certain that he had hidden his involvement by dealing through Galeazzo who in turn got most of the dirty work done by the Prior and other corruptibles.

Machiavelli, satisfied with himself for at least having deduced the motive for the scheme, if not the ultimate perpetrator, replied. "Vanity can often lead to a man's downfall. In this instance, it was your desire to have your image preserved on the walls of your own chapel. When you asked that young artist in to paint your chapel, that was the beginning of your end. He overheard you speaking of the need to be rid of the good Messer Corsini."

"Yes, I am sorry to say that your father-in-law's death was at the hands of one of my servants, who are sworn to secrecy when they enter my employ. I was amazed that you took the boy away, and I thought I had got away with it."

"You had," responded Machiavelli. "He claimed to be in love with your daughter, and did not want to ruin her through your demise. So he revealed nothing about what he had heard of your dealings. We had to let him go. But your second mistake was plotting to put an end to Michelangelo Buonarroti..."

"I did no such thing, until you stopped me just now," interrupted Benvenuti.

"But what about the poison that the Prior of San Miniato got some child to place amongst Michelangelo's paints?

"That was nothing to do with me. I have always admired great art, and would certainly not want such a talent extinguished. You see, I had commissioned him to paint my chapel, and promised him a substantial sum in payment. For no reason at all, well, some minor altercation with an unwelcome intruder on San Giovanni, he decided that my custom wasn't good enough for him. He'd just told me he was downing his tools when you walked in.

"My reaction, which you saw just now, I cannot explain. That same voice spoke to me, telling me that I could not tolerate his rejection of my contract, and the rage took hold. I barely know now what I was doing."

"Then the plan for Michelangelo's death must have been a private matter for the other person involved in your plans. We know about your involvement with Gianluca Galeazzo.

"Ah, Galeazzo, the simple fool. He was easily persuaded with a bit of money and the offer of a role as First Chancellor in my new republic.

"Be that as it may, Michelangelo's predecessor on your chapel contract came back here on San Giovanni. That is the intruder to whom you refer, is it not? He wanted to see Buonarroti, but was stopped by your staff, and kicked virtually to death in the *'altercation'* that you speak of. It was this which led to our discovery of your involvement.

"It is a shame that the boy looks likely to die to reveal the truth, but he gave us his diary in which he had written everything that he had observed whilst in your hospitality. We finally discovered what he knew about your involvement with Corsini. As you will know already, we arrested Gianluca Galeazzo. Unfortunately he was lynched and killed before we were able to extract any information from him. No doubt he would have told us that you were his paymaster.

"But it just needed one mention of his name on the same page as yours in the boy's diary to enable me to complete the chain, from the crimes, through the Prior of San Miniato and Galeazzo, to you. Why is it that you folk from the north think you can just walk into Florence and do whatever you want? You can't, our City is greater than all its opponents."

Benvenuti hung his head in shame. They took him back to the Signoria to obtain all the details. Machiavelli suspected that, given Benvenuti's current state of mind, the Strappado would prove unnecessary, as it had with the Prior.

On their way out, they passed Michelangelo who, for once, had been stunned into stillness by the ferocity of Benvenuti's attack and the narrowness of his escape from the jaws of death. "I would dispose of any current stocks of paints and dyes if I were you," Machiavelli told him. "I may be wrong about this, but I believe that the boy who was working for you planted some poison among them. I have no idea how that would work, as I do not imagine that you drink your paint, but to be safe, you should re-stock."

Although there was no way that word could have got out to the City about Benvenuti's involvement in the crime wave, Soderini did not want to risk another lynching, so he ordered the guards to take the prisoner in one of Benvenuti's own carriages rather than parading him through the streets for all to see.

Gonfaloniere Soderini and Niccolò Machiavelli led the way on their horses back to the Palazzo della Signoria. The Gonfaloniere reflected to his companion "Our City is a great city, Niccolò, and its capacity to surprise me never ceases."

"I love it more than my own soul," agreed Machiavelli.

"Just as the river that runs through it, the City carries on, and there is nothing that anyone can do to block her. As you said, it is a shame that the boy was brought to the point of death in order for us to solve the riddle that had been set for us, but that was just the City at work, preserving itself. I sometimes get the feeling it controls us all."

Machiavelli rode on in silence wondering whether the Gonfaloniere might be right. He had always believed that men controlled their surroundings, but Soderini had planted a seed of doubt in him. Could even the most powerful men's actions be dictated by the environment in which they found themselves?

CHAPTER 35

Donato awoke on a bed of straw. He felt awful – his bones ached all over his body, and he was nauseous. He lay still, trying to compose himself. After a while he forced his eyes open a crack, afraid that he might see hell around him.

Instead he recognised, with great relief, that he was in the downstairs room of Anziani's house. He closed his eyes again, and drifted back into unconsciousness.

Later, he woke again. As before, he could not open his eyes instantly, due to the waves of sickness that coursed through him. When they subsided a little, he once again forced his eyes open. This time, he saw Grazia looking over him. He tried to speak, but passed out with the effort.

Eventually, he came out of this limbo world, with Grazia hovering by his side. He managed to open his eyes more widely this time.

"Thank our Lady in heaven," whispered Grazia.

"We thought we'd lost you."

"What am I doing here?" asked Donato.

"You were brought here two weeks ago, in a terrible state. You have been in a fever since then. But you seem to have friends in high places now, as they sent the best doctor to tend to you. Even he, though, said that he did not expect you to make it. You must have had a strong will to live."

"Why, what happened to me?"

"Don't you remember? You were in *Le Stinche* after being set upon by that vile Benvenuti's servants. Apparently you were at death's door even when you arrived, but a day in that place is enough to kill anybody, let alone someone in your condition.

"But the angels must have been watching over you. The authorities decided to pardon you for whatever crime you were in there for. Someone must have found out that you knew Giovanni, and as he seems to be the only person you know in this City, they had you brought here. You couldn't move, so we made this little bed for you downstairs.

"Giovanni will be pleased to find that you have come round – I will send word to him straight away. But we are under strict orders to alert the Palazzo della Signoria as soon as you recover consciousness, so I don't imagine that you'll get much peace."

* * * * *

The next morning, Giovanni Anziani dutifully delivered the message to the government palace that

Donato had awoken. That very evening Second Chancellor Machiavelli arrived to talk to Donato.

"I have been asked by Gonfaloniere Soderini to give you his apologies that he was not able to come to see you this evening, due to pressing engagements of state. The City, and I personally, owe you a debt of thanks. I have no doubt that we would have got to the source of our crime-wave eventually, but it was only due to your diary and your observation that we were able to save one of our greatest artists from death in the nick of time."

Donato was not yet strong enough to engage in extensive conversation, as he was still barely able to eat, despite Grazia's best efforts at feeding him. He was curious, however, as to what had happened to him. "Thank you. But how did I end up here?"

"After I interviewed you in *Le Stinche* for the second time, you were taken back to your cell and took ill with a fever. A guard saw that you had a book in your hand, and took it for himself. I've no idea what he planned to do with it, as I am sure he would not have been able to read it. Luckily, the Captain of the prison saw him leave your cell with the book, and seized it. He took a quick look at it, and saw that it might be helpful to my investigation of the crime-wave.

"As soon as I started reading it, I realised that it was Benvenuti who was behind it all, and we got to his palace just in time to stop him killing Michelangelo. Needless to say, Benvenuti has been swiftly tried and executed."

"What about Chiara?" asked Donato.

"The family are still in their palace, but it is being

confiscated by the City and they will have to leave shortly. They are in disgrace, and I do not imagine they will be able to remain in Florence."

Donato was pained to hear he might never see Chiara again.

After a pause, he asked Machiavelli to carry on.

"It was clear from your diary that, apart from your dalliance with that girl, you are a good kid. The Gonfaloniere himself therefore decided that we should release you from *Le Stinche*, even though there were plenty of crimes that we could have held you for, such as disobeying my first order, adultery, and breaking into Benvenuti's palace.

"But nobody knew anything about you. Would you believe that it was Michelangelo, when he came to give a statement and we asked him about your encounter with him at the palace, who told us that you were friends with Anziani? So here we brought you, to be looked after by this good lady."

"Michelangelo did something for me? That's a good sign. When I am better, I will be sure to see him and maybe this time, if as you say I saved his life, he will give me the chance to work for him." Donato could not help seeing the positive in the situation, even though he still felt awful.

"I'm afraid that won't be possible," Machiavelli said with genuine regret. "The fact remains that you disregarded my order to leave the City. I would like to allow you to stay, according to Anziani you have potential as an artist. But I cannot let that happen, as it would undoubtedly lead to the questioning of my authority. I will therefore permit you to stay here until you are feeling better and able to move about, but then you must leave. If you do not do so this time, I shall have no choice but to have you executed."

Donato received the news that he would have to leave the City of his dreams like a dagger through his heart. He turned away from Machiavelli. "Then go."

EPILOGUE AND AUTHOR'S NOTE

Michelangelo went on to be one of the greatest artists the world has seen, although many of his most famous works, such as the frescoes in the Sistine Chapel in Rome, were done after he'd left Florence, as Italy's artistic focus moved south in the years that followed.

Due to Galeazzo's death before he could be interrogated, the involvement of Leonardo in the plot to kill his artistic rival was never discovered. He was in his fifties by the time of these events, and he carried on working for another fifteen years, spending most of that time back in Milan, Rome and France. In these later years, he moved away from art and worked more on his scientific and engineering endeavours.

Immediately after this episode, between late 1504 and 1506, both Leonardo and Michelangelo worked furiously on competing murals for the Salone dei Cinquecento in the Palazzo della Signoria. Although nothing remains of these commissions, they were extensively critiqued and copied, and many hold the opinion that they constituted the high point of renaissance art.

It is possible that the world lost an even greater artistic star with the expulsion of poor Donato from Florence.

* * * * *

The main storyline of this book is entirely fictional, but many of the characters in it are real, and they did and said many of the things attributed to them here, as revealed by contemporary diaries and letters. For example, Leonardo and Michelangelo really did have their unfriendly encounter near the Ponte a Santa Trinità. Machiavelli truly confessed (in a letter to his friend Luigi Guicciardini) to being tricked, in the circumstances described in chapter 15, into having sex with a woman so ugly it made him sick on her.

And, of course, Amerigo Vespucci really did make his famous journeys across the Atlantic. Although the lands had already been discovered by Christopher Columbus, many historians believe that it was not until Vespucci made his voyages that it was realised that the lands were not, as Columbus had believed, part of Asia, but instead constituted a whole new continent. That is how the continent came to bear Amerigo's name rather than that of his now more famous precursor.

Machiavelli and Leonardo did indeed collaborate on a project, between 1503 and 1506, to divert the River Arno away from Pisa in a bid to win Florence's ongoing war with its smaller neighbour. It is reported that

Leonardo's designs may have worked, but that the engineer placed in charge of executing his instructions altered the plans. As a result, the canals that were dug to take the water away from the river's current course were not deep enough, and the river quickly reverted to its original route. The project was then abandoned due to the manpower required to make it work properly being far beyond Florence's resources.

While Italians nowadays apply the name *'calcio'* to soccer, the game played in 1504 bore much more resemblance to rugby or even plain fighting. It had developed as a way to keep soldiers fit and strong, and was a highly physical contact sport. The only similarities to modern soccer are probably that the ball was round and that points were scored by getting the ball to a defined area at one end of the pitch. To this day, a game of *'calcio fiorentino'* is played in Piazza Santa Croce on the day of St John by teams of twenty-seven players each, and is almost as violent as the original.

A few other historical notes to put the story in context (the most avid historians may notice that I have had to 'bend' some timings to fit into the story, but these are only to a very small degree, and I apologise for any historical inaccuracy so caused)...

Although 'Italy' existed at that time as a geographical concept, it was made up of a large number of independent states, which often comprised little more than cities, such as Milan, Venice, Ferrara, Bologna, Lucca, Florence, Naples and the Papal States. These states frequently found themselves at war, either with each other or with other countries such as France. In 1504, a power struggle between France, which held Milan in the north, and Spain, which held Naples to the south, was being conducted over the territory in between, including Florence.

A century and a half previously, the Black Death was the biggest attack of plague in Europe, estimated to have killed around half of the continent's population. Even in the 1500s, the plague struck every ten years or so, killing hundreds of people in cities such as Florence. Understanding of disease was still very poor.

While Florence rightfully enjoyed a reputation as a beacon of learning in this age, that learning was confined to the privileged few. The reality is that probably around 90% of its inhabitants were illiterate.

The story is set in a time of great flux in the history of Florence, with regular and severe changes of regime. Arguably, 1504 was the zenith of the City's cultural standing, with Michelangelo's David and (probably) Leonardo's Mona Lisa being completed that year. This was also the year in which the other great artist of the era, Raphael, arrived in Florence for an extended stay from his native Urbino.

The City was a centre of academia, with the writings of ancient Greek and Roman philosophers holding considerable weight. Machiavelli, for example, was highly educated, and not the archetypal 'Machiavellian' that one might expect from the use of that epithet today.

The 'Machiavellian' label is derived almost entirely from his masterwork, 'The Prince', in which he described (rather than extolled) the qualities required to be a successful dictator in unsettled times. Far from supporting the idea of a ruthless individual leader as described in The

Prince, it is clear from his other writings that Machiavelli was a firm believer in republican government.

He was an accomplished diplomat, politician, historian, playwright and poet as well as a writer of prose, and was considerably more moderate and measured than his modern reputation suggests. The Prince, however misconstrued, remains influential to this day, not only giving us the 'Machiavellian' tag but also sayings such as 'the end justifies the means'.

Leonardo 'da' Vinci (the 'da' is a relatively modern addition to his name) had been commissioned by the City in 1503 to paint a great Florentine "Battle" scene on one wall of the Salone dei Cinquecento in the Palazzo della Signoria. In the second half of 1504, Machiavelli was behind Michelangelo receiving a similar commission for the opposite wall, prompting fevered activity and escalating enmity between the two great artists. Sadly, no remnants of the "Battles" remain – Leonardo's experimentation with paints went badly wrong and his Battle of Anghiari dissolved away, while Michelangelo's Battle of Cascina never got beyond the cartoon stage.

But the City's fortunes were on the wane. Ever since the death of Lorenzo "il Magnifico" Medici in 1492 (coincidentally the year of discovery of the 'Americas' by Columbus, an Italian, from Florence's rival city of Genova, but sailing under the flag of Spain), power in the Italian peninsular started to transfer to Rome. The Pope and his court had more money, and more inclination to use it.

Even though he was only in power for less than four years, the austerity imposed on the City by the "Mad Monk" Girolamo Savonarola greatly accelerated its decline, as rich families quickly moved their money to safer locations. It is perhaps fortunate that he was stopped and burnt in the same manner as he had used to destroy so many works of art and literature, on his Bonfires of the Vanities, lest Florence's cultural and artistic heritage be destroyed further.

Although the Medici family regained power over Florence in 1512 (following which Machiavelli was exiled, when he took the opportunity to write The Prince), the City continued to lose its importance both culturally and financially. Thus, having enjoyed its moment of ascendency as one of the most influential cities in the world, it became the ordinary, if beautiful, provincial city that exists today.

ABOUT THE AUTHOR

Justin Ellis was born in London in 1970. He grew up in England, Zambia, Indonesia and Italy, and now lives in Sussex in the south-east of England. He studied law at university, and has been a commercial solicitor in London since qualifying in 1995. In 2006 he was one of the founders of a new firm, iLaw. He likes to spend his spare time with his family and a glass of cold Manzanilla sherry in south-western Spain.

Death by the Arno is Justin's debut novel.

Printed in Dunstable, United Kingdom